AMERICAN HAVEN

Elizabeth Yates

JOURNEY
FORTH™

Greenville, South Carolina

Library of Congress Cataloging-in-Publication Data

Yates, Elizabeth, 1905-2001
  American haven / Elizabeth Yates.
    p. cm. — (Mountain adventures ; 3)
  Previously published under title: Haven for the brave. New York :
A.A. Knopf, 1941.
  Summary: Teenagers Michael and Meredith Lamb find new
friends and mountains to climb when they travel from war-torn Lon-
don to New Hampshire with their Uncle Tony during World War II.
  ISBN 1-57924-896-9 (alk. paper)
  [1. Brothers and sisters—Fiction. 2. Uncles—Fiction. 3. World War,
1939-1945—Fiction. 4. Mountaineering—Fiction. 5. New Hampshire—Fiction.] I. Title.
  PZ7.Y213 Am 2002
    [Fic]—dc21

2002009142

American Haven

Elizabeth Yates

Designed by Miin ng
Cover and illustrations by John Roberts
Edited by Andrea Ruffner

ISBN 1-57924-880-2

15 14 13 12 11 10 9 8 7 6 5 4 3 2 1

Books by Elizabeth Yates

Amos Fortune, Free Man
Carolina's Courage
The Journeyman
Hue & Cry
Sound Friendships
The Next Fine Day
Mountain Born
A Place for Peter
Sarah Whitcher's Story
Someday You'll Write

Mountain Adventures series
Swiss Holiday
Iceland Adventure
American Haven

Contents

US 2

Mt. Adams

PRESIDENTIAL R

Mt. Jefferson

Great G

Gulfside
Trail

Mt. Clay

Mt. Washington
Cog Railway

Summit
House

Mt. Was

Ammonoosuc Ravine Trail

Lakes of the
Clouds Hut

Lion

Base Station

Boott
Spur

PRESIDENTIAL RANGE

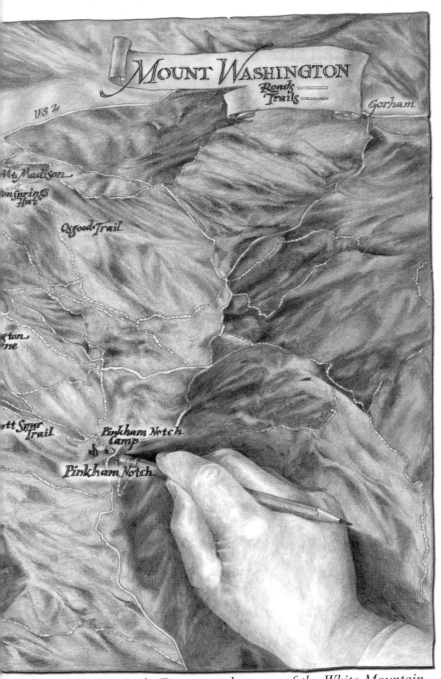

At lunch, Uncle Tony spread a map of the White Mountain National Forest on the table and pointed to Pinkham Notch with his pencil.

Chapter 1

War in England

London, 1940

"Uncle Tony is coming for tea this afternoon, Meredith, so come right home from school."

"I shall, Mum." Merry leaned over and kissed her mother goodbye. "When is he going to America?"

"He doesn't know. Perhaps any minute. Whenever he hears that his boat is sailing. I do wish that you—"

"Oh, Mum," Merry exclaimed quickly, "I'll be late if I don't hurry." She turned to her father. "Daddy, will you be home in time for some tennis this afternoon?"

He nodded. "Let's meet in the gardens at six o'clock. We'll have a good hour then."

Merry kissed his cheek and left the house quickly, running along the sidewalk as she hurried off to school.

Inside the house, Merry's mother went on with her unfinished sentence. "I do wish that we could persuade Merry and Michael to go to America with your brother when he goes."

"They seem determined to stay here with us," Mr. Lamb replied quietly. "But I'm afraid that soon they're going to have to go to America whether they wish to or not."

Mr. and Mrs. Lamb looked at each other across the table. It was strange, this time of war that made parents send their children to unknown homes thousands of miles away for uncertain lengths of time.

"They've missed so many days of school," Mrs. Lamb went on. "And there's no chance of a holiday with all the beaches closed."

"If a holiday is all the children miss this year, it isn't much to worry about." Mr. Lamb smiled as he rose from the table. "Who knows, perhaps Tony can persuade them to go with him before we have to insist that they go."

"I'm glad we got their passports," Mrs. Lamb said.

"I just hope they understand," Mr. Lamb concluded.

They soon went their separate ways—Mr. Lamb to the office, and Mrs. Lamb to the shops, carrying the family's ration books. Meals were harder to plan these days, but the family had not suffered.

As she shopped, Mrs. Lamb thought about her two children. Michael would soon be sixteen, and he was already counting the years until he might join the Royal Air Force. Merry, nearly fifteen, was tall for her age, with burnished blonde hair and deep brown eyes. The past year of war had made her silent more often, and her face was strained when news came over the radio or someone read from the paper. But neither she nor Michael would hear of leaving their parents for America.

"We won't change our minds, Mum," they often protested when their mother urged them to reconsider. "We far prefer to stay with you and see things through."

As Mrs. Lamb walked, she turned her eyes away from the pavement with its white paint to guide people during the evening blackouts, the shop windows with criss-crossed paper to prevent shattering, and the sandbags and barbed wire embellishing the street. Instead, she focused her attention on the blue August sky above. As she looked up, she prayed, as many did so often these days, that the sky would not fall.

At school, Merry worked hard on her lessons all morning. After lunch, Miss Robbins suggested that the class go for an hour's walk. Merry would have much preferred to keep working in order to go home early. She wanted to be at home very much these days. Although the war had brought only a few adjustments to daily life such as blackouts and no sugar, life had become like a picture that was now a little blurry. And no matter how one tried, it could not be brought back into focus.

"Where's Daphne?" Merry asked in the cloakroom as the girls were putting on their hats.

"Gone to America," Irene answered. "She's had her trunk packed for three months, ever since her mother was told that Daphne might have to leave with only twenty-four hours' notice. I think Daphne's rather fortunate. I wish I could go to America."

"Why?" Merry asked, surprised.

"Because I want to be a math teacher when I finish school—that'll be in just two more years—and if we learn as little in the next two years as we have in this past one, I'll never pass my first exams."

"Oh." Merry had never thought of it quite that way. The war had interrupted many of their school days.

Merry didn't want to go to America because she wanted to be strong enough to face whatever rigors the war put upon her and share the burden with her family. But now she saw that perhaps she might be able to serve England better if she got on with her education and left heroics to those better qualified than she.

Yesterday, Daphne had been at school, cheerful, noisy, and exuberant. Today, all that remained was her cardboard gas-mask carrier hanging on its hook. Merry smiled, remembering the day when they had practiced a drill. At the word "Gas!" everyone had taken a deep breath and donned their masks. Daphne had started giggling so hard that she had broken the isinglass windows.

Merry and Irene and Phyllis chatted and laughed as they walked to the park. As they reached the gates, the girls spotted a fruit peddler with a cart filled to the brim with ripe plums.

"Straight from Evesham, lovely plums, won't see their like again, not this year, young ladies," he called out. "Lovely plums from Evesham!"

"First find our place in the park, girls," Miss Robbins called out to the excited students, "then someone can come back for fruit."

The girls raced across the grass to a massive beech that had been adopted long ago as the school tree. On its trunk was a small, neat sign with an arrow—TO THE AIR RAID SHELTER, ONE MINUTE. The girls arranged themselves comfortably under the tree and brought out their needlework. Miss Robbins pulled out a book to read aloud while they worked.

"Meredith, you may go back and buy a basket of plums," Miss Robbins said. Merry quickly collected the coppers and sixpences from the others, then headed back to the fruit peddler and his plums.

While she waited, she petted the peddler's horse and listened to a street musician who was playing his harp nearby. The haunting loveliness of "Londonderry Air" drifted around her. The peddler handed Merry her plums; she crossed the street and stood beside the musician. When he finished, she pulled a sixpence from her pocket.

"This is for your dog," she said, motioning to the brown ball of fur that lay at the man's feet. "Will you get him a bone tonight from me?"

"That I will, young lady," he smiled. "Now, what tune would you like to hear?"

"The 'Londonderry Air' again, please." The man's fingers began the wistful melody again, and Merry laid a few extra coppers in his battered hat.

As Merry walked back to the park, she thought that perhaps she should purchase a few extra plums. While the peddler measured out more fruit, she stroked the horse's ears in time to the music.

Suddenly there came the shattering wail of the air raid siren—rising, falling, invading every corner of quietness. Merry stared wide-eyed at the peddler. For an instant, neither could decide what to do. Across the park, Miss Robbins and the girls gathered together to flee to the shelter. Miss Robbins called shrilly to Merry. Merry opened her mouth to answer, but no words came out. It was like trying to call out in a dream.

The peddler was the first to move. "Give us a hand, miss, and help me unhitch old Bess."

Propelled into action, Merry started undoing the harness with trembling fingers. "Wh-why?" she asked through stiff lips.

"Orders, miss. When the siren sounds, all horses are to be loosed from their posts and tied to the carts or led to safety." His words came with steady calm.

With a suddenness like the clap of thunder after the lightning's warning, there were planes roaring overhead. While the siren's wail rose and fell, the harpist across the street kept fingering out his tune.

The peddler pointed to a doorway across the street. Merry ran to it and pressed herself against the wall, shivering uncontrollably. The peddler followed her to the shelter. Old Bess joined them, her bony sides pressing against them both. Just then, a plane dived so low that its swastika was discernable.

The peddler stroked the old horse. "The bomb that's got Bess's name on it has mine, too," he said. "We've been together some twenty years, and old Hitler isn't going to separate us now."

With a suddenness like the clap of thunder after the light-ning's warning, there were planes roaring overhead.

The air was full of the noise of antiaircraft barrage, the zoom of bombers, the rattle of machine guns, and the crashing of bombs. Merry heard the quick rush of British fighter planes soaring into the air to drive off the invaders. And although her hands were pressed tightly over her eyes, she saw them in her mind.

There was a lull for a moment. It was horrid, this feeling that her heart had gone to water. Merry peered out around Bess's brown body. The street was full of rubble. There was a gaping hole where the park gates had stood. There was no more music coming from the harp, for it now lay in the street with its strings reaching jaggedly into the air. Beside it was something that looked like a bundle of old clothes. Nearby, a little brown dog was whimpering. Merry dashed across the street to the dog. She pulled him into her arms and darted back to the wall while the planes went roaring overhead.

"You've got a lot of nerve, miss!" the peddler exclaimed. Merry tightly clutched the dog to herself to still the wild beating of his heart against her own.

The noise was lessening now, getting higher and farther away. Merry buried her head in the little dog's fur. *What waste, what needless destruction*, she thought bitterly. An anguish of hate rose in her against the evil that could cause such suffering in the world. Suddenly she knew why fathers and mothers wanted their children to go to America. The air had become hauntingly still. The silence was broken by the lilting sound of the all-clear signal.

Merry and the peddler stepped down from the doorway. The peddler, seeing that there was no longer any cart loaded with Evesham plums, put his hand on Bess's bridle.

"Cheerio, miss," he said, and he started away, whistling as he led the old horse down the street.

"Goodbye—and thank you," Merry called after him, finding her tongue.

A warden appeared and knelt beside the bundle of clothes near the harp. Merry went over to him.

"Is he—" It was hard to say the word. "Is he—dead?" she asked, a matter-of-fact tone in her voice that startled her.

The warden looked up at her. "Yes. Do you know anything about him?"

"Only that he had a dog."

The warden smiled sadly at the small creature still shivering in Merry's arms. "Can you give him a home now?"

"Yes, of course," Merry exclaimed. She was glad to have something to do.

Miss Robbins and the girls came quickly across the park. "Meredith Lamb, that was wrong of you not to come with us," Miss Robbins said as she came toward Merry and the warden. "However, I am very relieved that you're safe." Miss Robbins looked at her watch, then at her students. "Now, girls, each one of you hurry to your homes as quickly as you can. And please be careful!"

An hour later, Merry reached home. Everyone knew that London had experienced its first real air raid. No one was sure what damage had been done, but that worry was offset by the assurance that none of the invading planes had returned to their bases.

Merry pushed open the front door and found her parents and her Uncle Tony sitting in the front room. They all turned toward her as she entered. Merry was pale, and her hat was pushed back on her head. Under one arm was a brown dog.

"Meredith!" Her mother rushed to her. "I'm so glad you're safe! We've been telephoning the school ever since we knew the raid was over south London, but we couldn't get any answer."

"I'm all right," Merry said quietly. "Everyone's all right, I think."

"Did you see what happened?" her father asked.

"A few things went on overhead. I don't know what really happened." She smiled thinly. She tried to answer the questions her parents asked, but the words seemed to be stuck in her throat. She shook her head, then turned to her father. "Am I too late for that game of tennis, Daddy?"

Uncle Tony leaped from his chair. "I'll give you a game before supper, Merry. But first—" He looked pointedly at the bundle of brown fur in Merry's arms.

"Oh," Merry smiled, "he's *my* dog now. Daddy, could you please take care of him while Uncle Tony and I play?"

"Where did you get him, Merry?" her father asked as she laid the limp bundle into his arms.

Far off in Merry's thoughts she could hear the strains of "Londonderry Air," louder than the whine of bombs and the thud of falling bricks.

"He was given to me this afternoon. I think we should call him Pippin. I may keep him, mayn't I?" she begged.

"He's a rather mouldy affair," Daddy began."If there's one thing he needs, it's a bath. After that, perhaps we can begin to make something civilized out of him."

"He seems hungry," Mum said. "Let me feed him first."

Merry seized Uncle Tony by the hand and dragged him from the room, leaving her father and mother contemplating Pippin with raised eyebrows.

Uncle Tony beat Merry so badly in the first set that he went up to her at the net to ask what was the matter.

"When are you going to America?" she asked in reply.

"When the government gives me my orders. Perhaps tonight, perhaps next week," he replied lightly, surprised at her interest.

She lowered her voice. "Uncle Tony, I want so terribly to see Michael. Couldn't you take me down to his school? Daddy gave the car up ages ago, but you've still got some petrol, haven't you?"

Uncle Tony looked at Merry, knowing this was more than a whim. "We might drive down tomorrow, first thing in the afternoon," he said slowly. "I'll collect you after school."

Merry threw her arms around his neck. "You won't beat me this game," she cried, challenging him. She picked up her racket and ball and ran back to the serving line. And he didn't.

When they returned to the house for supper, they were greeted at the door by a brown whirlwind of fur. Daddy emerged from the basement, a huge wet apron enveloping him.

"Pippin is quite a respectable creature, Merry," he said approvingly. "A Welsh terrier, I should say. He was so dirty and his hair was so matted that I had to wash him three times."

"He was quite hungry, as well. You'd think he hadn't eaten in a week," Merry's mother added.

"Thank you for washing him and doing everything for him." Merry pulled Pippin into her arms, and the brown whirlwind settled down to peace and home.

The next afternoon, Merry was off to Michael's school with Uncle Tony. He had promised her an hour with her brother without asking what she wanted it for. He would have tea with Michael's headmaster, who happened to be one of his particular friends.

Many of the boys in Michael's school had gone home on holiday if their homes were in the country. Those who lived in the cities or "dangerous areas" had remained on at the school to do special work or make up time lost in the past winter. Uncle Tony and Merry found Michael hoeing in the school garden. He was pleased although rather surprised to see them. Uncle Tony went off to Mr. Davies's house, and Merry suggested going for a walk.

"Uncle Tony gave me a half crown so we could have tea in the village. Mr. Davies said you could go," Merry explained.

They hurried across the fields to a small shop where they ordered tea and crumpets. Merry poured the tea the way she knew Michael liked it, hesitating over the sugar. He shook his head. "That's not too hard to go without," he said.

"Did you have any excitement yesterday?" Merry asked quietly.

"A spot of bother," he said. "Didn't get any damage though, just got people's wind up a bit."

Even with his sister, Michael was discreet. After a raid, one was not supposed to tell what damage there was or where it had occurred, as the enemy might learn valuable information. But they had shared too many things for Michael not to share this also, so leaning further over the table and talking in lowered tones, he went on.

"We were having an algebra lesson when there came a colossal bang. Everything shook, and the windows rattled. Professor Mosey went as white as chalk, but he told us to get down between our desks. Fairfax Minor said something funny—he always does, you know—and we started laughing so that we hardly heard anything else. There were some awful thuds though, and it made my ears feel as if I'd been up in a plane."

"Where were the thuds?"

"In a field. My professor said later that the Germans often drop their bombs anywhere so that when they get home they can say that so many bombs were dropped and great damage was done."

Merry looked hard at Michael, then she said quickly, "Let's go to America with Uncle Tony. We've got our passports, and he'll take us."

Michael stared at her. "Meredith Lamb, how can you change? Last time I saw you, nothing would drag you to America. Now, what's come over you? You're not going chicken-hearted are you?"

"Oh, no, Michael!" she denied, horrified at his accusation.

"Oh, I say, Merry, I'm sorry," he said. "I heard the raiders were over south London yesterday, but they said it was late afternoon, and I thought you were probably home from school."

Merry soon told Michael all about the previous day's experience. The words spilled from her lips as Michael listened, his eyes growing round. A smile spread over his face at the news of Pippin.

"I'm not afraid of anything, Michael," Merry said earnestly. "It isn't fear I feel, even when my heart does go to water, but—Michael, I don't want to grow up hating things. Daddy once said that was the worst thing that could happen to anyone. And I—I can't help but hate during something like yesterday."

"I know how you feel," Michael said.

"Mum and Daddy want us to go to America. Uncle Tony can take us when he goes. His friends are willing to have us stay with them. Aren't we rather fortunate to have such opportunities?"

"I've rather wanted to go to America all along," Michael reminded her gently. "School work is so interrupted here that I'd like the chance to be someplace where I could carry on steadily. But you were so against it, Merry, and I knew we had to stick together on things."

Now there was hardly time for anything except finishing their tea, for their boat might sail tomorrow. They were soon racing back across the fields to Mr. Davies's house. They found Uncle Tony and the headmaster in the study chatting over tea.

"Uncle Tony," Merry burst out, "we're going to America with you if you'll still take us."

"Wonderful!" Uncle Tony exclaimed. He turned to the confused headmaster. "I'm going to America on a government commission, and some friends of mine in New England have opened their home to any pair of British youngsters that I can bring with me."

"I'm glad to hear that," the headmaster replied, "but is there really such a rush? Couldn't Michael wait and go up to London this weekend in the ordinary way?"

Uncle Tony shook his head. "You see, we don't know— the boat may sail tonight or next week, and we've got to be ready to go."

"I understand," the headmaster murmured. He excused Michael to go pack, and Merry listened quietly to Uncle Tony and the headmaster.

"But what about their schooling, Antony? Michael is doing well in chemistry, and he may have a future before him in that line of work. I shouldn't like to think of his work being interrupted—"

"Davies," Uncle Tony broke in, "I can't promise you that Michael will carry on in America as he does here. My friends live in a small town, and the local school will be the best that can be offered, but all things considered—"

"I'm sure Michael will learn in other ways," the headmaster conceded. "I'm glad he is going." He turned to Merry. "He means a lot to you, doesn't he?"

She nodded solemnly.

Michael joined them, bags and boxes in hand. They left the room and went out to Uncle Tony's car.

"And you both mean a lot to Britain," the headmaster continued. "You will each be an ambassador of sorts. No matter how long you are away, never forget the country you are representing and the one to which you will return. There is the bravery of those who go into battle, and the bravery of those who stay at home to guard the fortress, and there is the bravery of those who see that their work lies in the future." The headmaster shook hands with them both.

"Thank you, sir, and goodbye," Michael said. He looked up at the ivy-covered stone walls, wondering when he would see them again. Soon they were climbing into the car and waving farewell to the headmaster and Michael's schoolmates who had come out to see him off. Then they were off on the road to London.

Chapter 2

Thumbs Up!

It did not take long to pack everything for the journey. There was a limit to the luggage they could take—warm and useful clothes, but nothing in excess. The only extras Mum allowed were their mountain climbing outfits. They went shopping in Oxford Street and purchased a black suit for Michael and a gray dress for Merry. If they did not grow too much, Michael and Merry would be decently and sensibly clad for the upcoming year.

Even in the midst of a war, London seemed to stay the same. Red buses rolled through the streets in the same easy way. The gardens were lovelier than ever with multi-colored masses of dahlias replacing the summer flowers. Shops were bustling with crowds, people were friendly. For the first time, Michael and Merry realized how important these familiar things were to them. At home, a common thing such as sitting around the table with Mum and Daddy was now a meaningful experience. There seemed to be so much to say, but often they could not find the right words.

Michael began teaching Pippin to respond to his commands and announced the dog's progress every evening at supper. Uncle Tony came for tennis almost every afternoon. Two large cases, packed and sitting by the front door, were the only reminders that life would soon change.

One night the telephone rang shrilly, waking the entire household. Merry heard Daddy fumbling down the dark hallway to answer it. "All right, Tony. We'll get them up." His voice seemed loud in the quiet house. "When did you say? We'll be ready."

Merry's heart began to race, the immensity of their whole adventure sweeping over her in a wave. She lay very still in her warm bed. Daddy went into Michael's room, and Merry heard their sentences, slow and quiet and deep. She heard Michael jumping from bed and Daddy coming down the hall to her room. Then he was standing beside her, and the night was still around them. He put out his hand to wake her.

"I'm awake, Daddy," she said, grasping his hand and pulling him down to sit beside her on the edge of the bed.

"Merry, do you remember what you learned on Sunday? 'It all depends on me, and I depend on God.' " Daddy's voice was quiet and solemn. "Let's keep that as our watchword, you and Michael, Mum and me. If we do, I think we'll find that we aren't so far apart as the ocean would make us seem."

"Oh, Daddy, war is horrible," Merry said with a tight throat. It was only war that was causing this parting.

"It is," he agreed. "Promise me something?"

"Anything."

"Never let yourself hate anything or anybody no matter what happens—to Mum or me, to London, to the world. Never stoop so low as to hate. Hate is worse than all the bombs in the world—it kills souls while they only kill bodies."

"I promise, Daddy," Merry said solemnly. She reached up and hugged him tightly.

Daddy left the room, and Mum soon came in, drawing the heavy curtains at the window so the light could be turned on. Merry sat up in bed and sipped at the steaming cup of cocoa that Mum handed her. She looked over the rim at Mum, so trim in her dark hat and coat, her eyes large in her pale face. Suddenly Merry saw her as she had never seen her before.

"How beautiful you are, Mum!" she exclaimed.

Mum laughed and urged Merry to hurry. "Uncle Tony said he would be along in less than an hour."

Merry drank her cocoa quickly and jumped from her bed to dress while Mum chatted, admonishing Merry to be useful in the new home she was going to. Mum adjusted Merry's outfit as she talked, patting a fold here, straightening a tuck there. She stepped back, pleased with her tall, slim daughter ready for a journey into the unknown.

"I'm proud of you, Merry, and I expect I'll be a good bit prouder when you return."

Merry threw her arms around her mother. What was it that made you see things as wonderful just when you were leaving them, as if only then you saw them in their true light?

Merry heard the muffled beat of a taxicab's engine out in the street. The doorbell jangled throughout the house as Merry and Mum came down the stairs. Pippin tried to block the door, ears laid back and one paw up.

"We'll take good care of him," Daddy said.

"Come along, Pippin," Mum called, starting toward the kitchen.

Pippin made no move except to look up at Michael and Merry. Merry dropped on her knees and picked up the small dog.

"He has to come with us," she said. "He was given to me as a very special charge."

There seemed a hundred reasons why Pippin should be left at home, but with the taxi outside and Uncle Tony on the doorstep there was no time to give them. Pippin settled down contentedly in Merry's arms, and they all went out into the dark street. Daddy and Uncle Tony hoisted the luggage onto the top of the taxi before they all climbed into the taxi. They drove slowly through the black, quiet streets, the tiny slits of headlights the taxi was allowed to show doing almost nothing to pierce the darkness.

The station was dimly lit, and shadowy figures moved about—soldiers, airmen, canteen girls offering cups of tea and coffee. There was a great crowd of people around the train and a band playing "There'll Always Be an England."

Final farewells were exchanged, then Merry, Michael, and Uncle Tony quickly boarded the train. The train began to pull away slowly. The passengers seemed to be shadows moving into an uncertain world, waving to other shadows on the platform. No one knew when the shadows would look into each other's faces again, or what would happen to them in the days or years that lay between.

"Thumbs up!" a shrill Cockney voice shouted.

A cheer echoed through the train and along the platform as many thumbed-up hands waved goodbye. The station slowly faded from view as the long train disappeared into the night.

Several hours after daybreak, they reached the docks their ship would sail from. Uncle Tony suggested that they eat breakfast in a small café nearby since they had some time before they would sail. They could see the ship in the distance, a dark gray mass looming against a gray sky.

After breakfast, they walked toward the gangplank where passengers were beginning to gather. Foreign tongues filled the air. Men and women in uniform stood about the dock, mingling with tin-hatted policemen and children of various ages. Laughter echoed, and the air was alive with excitement.

Uncle Tony greeted a group of quiet-voiced, serious-faced businessmen and preceded Michael and Merry up the gangplank. Merry followed, holding Pippin tightly in her arms, and Michael held out their passports to the official in charge. The official stamped the passports, then put his hand into his pocket. "Hold on, miss. I've got a present for you and one for your brother, too." He handed each of them a small book.

"Thank you, sir," Merry and Michael said in unison.

"Don't thank me. The Committee in London is responsible for that book. They're giving one to every British boy and girl who leaves these shores. Now then, good speed to you—and come back soon."

The books contained prose and poetry for "the children of the defenders of freedom who set sail from Great Britain in 1940." Their names were printed inside the books as well.

The ship began hooting softly as the engines started up. There were shouts on the dock as the gangplank was wheeled away and the ship edged away from the quay. Somewhere a band began playing. The travelers on board the ship and friends on the shore shot their thumbs up into the air in a confident, cheerful gesture. People waved, shouting final words across the widening water.

As the band began to play "God Save the King," everyone stood at attention. The space of water grew larger, and almost before one noticed, England became as dim and indistinct as the strains of music. The ship moved quickly, its gray hulk merging with the gray of the ocean.

Later that afternoon a bell rang, and passengers gathered on the starboard deck for Boat Drill. As they donned belts and life jackets, the sailors demonstrated how to board the lifeboats if—. Everything hung on that small word—"if." An officer gave instructions in a casual voice, just as if he were reading market reports. If they were torpedoed, they were to do this; if they were bombed from the air, they were to do that; if they were machine-gunned, they were to do something else. All orders were to be obeyed instantly. There were to be no lights after dark.

"And we all hope you have a very pleasant voyage," he concluded. Merry bit her lip to keep from laughing at the incongruity of it all.

"Can you two look after yourselves until lunch?" Uncle Tony asked. "I have a meeting in the cabin."

"Certainly," Michael said. "We'll meet you in the dining room when the bell rings."

Uncle Tony smiled, then walked away with the group of serious business men.

Michael and Merry did not ask Uncle Tony why he was going to America. One did not ask questions in England these days, especially of someone in government service.

Merry looked back over the water. All she could make out was a faint dark bar, greener than the gray-green of the ocean. That was England. All she loved was back there. Ahead of her lay a mystery. Merry remembered studying about the English Pilgrims who had crossed this same ocean long ago. Now she and Michael and all the others were pilgrims on this dark sea.

Michael pulled out the book from the Committee of London. He opened it and read in a quiet voice,

> *This England never did, nor never shall,*
> *Lie at the proud foot of a conquerer . . .*
> *Come the three corners of the world in arms,*
> *And we shall shock them. Naught shall make us rue,*
> *If England to itself do rest but true.*

There was a long silence, broken only by the swishing of water against the ship's side and the whistle of the wind.

"I don't think Americans will be that different after all," Michael said. "No matter what else separates us, we have one thing in common—we all value freedom."

Merry smiled at him. His words calmed her. A whole nation of people opening their homes to a lot of strangers was something to marvel at.

Chapter 3

A World with Lights

The day finally came when everyone breathed more easily. At last, the Atlantic Ocean with its uncertainties underneath and overhead was behind them. Before them, rising faintly out of the water, was a blue line of land—Canada.

The ship entered the St. Lawrence waterway. As the river narrowed, Michael and Merry could see both its banks—the tall Laurentian Mountains on the northern side and the hills of pine trees on the southern side with small villages and farms at their base. As evening began to darken the sky, the ship drew near Quebec where it would land. The city bustled with life. Trains moved close to the water, ferries sailed back and forth, smoke curled from tall chimneys. The city towered above them. At first the lights gleamed here and there like fireflies in the twilight, but as the ship edged nearer, the city seemed to blaze with lights.

They landed and passed quickly through the officials at the dock. Taxis honked their horns, eager for business, and a row of high-wheeled, old-fashioned carriages stood along the dock. Uncle Tony hailed one, and they climbed in after he arranged to have their luggage sent to the hotel ahead of them. The driver spoke a curious mixture of French and English as he talked to them and to his horse, slapping the reins ineffectually over its broad back. They jogged along over the cobbles, winding up the narrow streets with their French signs, past the little shops—*patisserie, boucherie, libraire*—to the maze of clustered houses and pointed steeples in the upper part of the city.

"All these lights, Uncle Tony!" Merry exclaimed. "I can't believe they're real!" Because of the blackouts in London,

Here in Quebec, lights were everywhere, blazing and beautiful.

they had not seen light anywhere after sunset except indoors behind heavy, black curtains. But here in Quebec, lights were everywhere, blazing and beautiful.

Dinner at the hotel was a feast, and the three British travelers ordered things whose taste they had forgotten. When one pat of butter was used, another was put down beside it. The sugar bowl overflowed with lumps, so it was quite all right to take extras to feed the horses.

The next morning, Uncle Tony went off for meetings, so Michael and Merry explored the city, discovering quaint streets and beautiful monuments. They ate lunch in a little *confiserie*, then walked along broad Dufferin Terrace. From there, they could look down on the activity of the lower town and across the St. Lawrence River to the shores of the Ile d'Orleans, a large island in the middle of the river. Voices filled the air around them, excited strains of French as well as many forms of accented English.

Uncle Tony was waiting for them when they returned to the hotel. He ordered tea and toast and plenty of jam to be sent up to their room. As they ate, he filled them in on his plans. They would not cross the border into the United States for a week because he had to confer with several officials in Quebec.

"I was talking with a friend today," Uncle Tony went on, "and he suggested that you'd be much happier on the Ile d'Orleans. He knows a family you can stay with and is making all the arrangements. You'll have to speak French, I expect, but that ought to be good for you. We'll have to leave tonight though, because I have to leave early in the morning."

Merry and Michael packed quickly, and soon they were driving with Uncle Tony and his friend alongside the river. They crossed a long, graceful bridge embellished with lights and drove onto the Ile d'Orleans. The windows of little white houses glowed with lamplight. The villages were serene and tidy, each one dominated by a red-roofed church. Finally, they came to the village where Merry and Michael would stay. Uncle Tony's friend stopped the car in front of a farmhouse separated from the road by a garden filled with flowers and vegetables. The house was hung with vines, and its roof swooped down gracefully over the gleaming windows.

The LaFlamme family came out of the house to meet them. There were Monsieur and Madame LaFlamme, their son André and his wife Nicole, their daughter Celeste and her husband Pierre, and several grandchildren of varying ages. Excited chattering and greetings made Michael and Merry feel quite welcomed, but all too soon they had to say goodbye to Uncle Tony.

Madame LaFlamme and Celeste took Michael and Merry upstairs to their rooms. Each one was spotless and shiny, looking as if it were freshly painted. Bright handloomed rugs covered the bare floors. Nicole brought them each a warm glass of milk, and before the clock in the tall village church struck ten, Michael and Merry were asleep.

Michael woke early the next morning and lay still for several moments, wondering where he was. There had been so many different beds lately—the ship, the hotel in Quebec, and now this small iron bed with its hand-woven blankets. The sun, shining through the slats of the closed shutters, lay in bars of light along the floor. Michael heard the clop of horses' hooves going along a road. A bell began ringing. Suddenly, Michael remembered where he was—on the Ile d'Orleans, in the French home they had come to last night. He jumped out of bed and dressed quickly.

Michael went out to the garden with Pippin, and Merry soon joined him. A little while later, Madame LaFlamme called, "*Le petit dejeuner, le petit dejeuner,*" and Michael and Merry ran inside to join the family at breakfast. There were many good things to eat and a great deal to say, so a flow of talk was soon racing around the table. The conversation revolved around the many jobs to be done that day and which were most urgent—potato digging, getting the eels, preparing the vegetables for market. Michael and Merry offered to help, and the family was delighted to secure two extra pairs of hands.

Madame LaFlamme served Michael and Merry a second helping of eggs while André told them about the island.

"We live as those before us lived," André explained. "Very little has changed. We have good farmland here—very fertile and rich. There is excellent fishing here as well. Most of the villages around the island have the same names as their churches—such as St. Petronille, St. Laurent, and St. Francois. Most of the houses are whitewashed stone with sloping roofs so that in winter the snow will fall to the ground."

"Almost every house has a loom," Celeste added, pointing to her own in the corner of the large room. "Many of the islanders are great weavers, and in the winter they spin and dye and weave fabrics the same way as other generations have done."

After breakfast, Merry walked alongside a slow-moving pair of oxen to the potato field while Michael went down to the river with the men of the family. The men had set eel traps the day before and the catch would determine whether a trip to the market would be profitable or not. André gave Michael a line of his own to pull on, and they busied themselves collecting the creatures that looked like enormous worms.

Michael played his line lightly, looking up every now and then across the sloping meadows to the high brown field where the women were digging potatoes, bent figures straightening up and doubling over. After a year of living in the midst of war—blackouts, restrictions, raids—it seemed that Ile d'Orleans was the picture of peace. There was always work to be done with the land, enough food for the family's needs and some left over to sell, and life going on with little change over the centuries. The rest of the world might go its way of progress or destruction, but here on the island was peace.

Pippin's excited barking pulled Michael's mind back to his task. Something was struggling on the end of his line. He played it for awhile, then slowly heaved it in. It was like dragging a rock from the sea. Michael moved steadily up on the eel, inching himself into the water even as he inched the eel nearer to the shore. The men, packing their eels into baskets, left their work to watch Michael and called suggestions to him. Thirty minutes later, Michael had landed a monster eel. The Quebecois shouted their admiration and approval as they gathered around Michael.

"*Oh la la! Comme il est grand!*" André exclaimed.

"*C'est un tresor, peut-etre deux dollars aux marche!*"

"I wish we could let the others know about this prize," André said, looking across the fields.

Michael's mind seized upon an idea, and he called Pippin to his side. Quickly he scribbled a note on a piece of paper and tied it to Pippin's collar. He knelt down and took Pippin's head between his hands and spoke slowly, looking straight into the dog's brown eyes.

"Take it to Merry," he commanded slowly. He repeated the command and added a firm push. Pippin looked up the sloping land where Michael pointed. He stood poised for a moment, then doubled his legs under him and began to cover the distance. The men watched him go up the lane and across the fields.

Pippin stopped in front of the empty house and waited hopefully. Michael's heart sank. It was a new experiment, a new command, but Pippin knew Merry's name, and Michael had thought he'd be able to find her. As the men attempted to predict the outcome, Michael held his breath in eagerness.

Pippin backed away from the house and put his nose to the ground, dashing back and forth across the road. Finally he seemed to pick up the track that the ox cart had taken earlier that morning. He ran down the road, turned at the lane, entered the field, and raced across the rough earth to where Merry and the other potato diggers were hard at work.

"Bravo!" André cried. *"Il l'a trouvee!"*

Michael beamed, more thrilled about Pippin's success than the landing of the eel. He could see Merry reading the note and telling the others in the field. He watched as the potato workers put their heads together. Merry wrote a note and tied it to Pippin's collar.

Soon Pippin was flying across the fields again toward Michael. André untied the note and handed it to Michael before congratulating the panting dog. Michael read the note aloud to the others.

Congratulations! Celeste says we shall have a party tonight to celebrate, Merry had written. The men waved jubilantly to the women in the field.

News spread quickly around the island about the party. That afternoon, the men went to the fields alone while the women worked in the warm, roomy kitchen preparing the food for the evening.

At eight o'clock, darkness began to fall. Merry lit the lamps, and logs crackled in the fireplace. The LaFlamme family, wearing their best black clothing, sat by the stove, their round cheeks shining like apples and their dark hair plastered smooth to their heads.

Soon the guests began to gather from all over the island with the clop of horses' hooves and the crunch of carriage wheels. The fiddler took his place by the stove. The music was so bright that his feet often led him around the room, weaving in and out among the dancing couples. Michael and Merry sang along with the Quebecois whose hearty voices filled the room with cheerfulness.

In the middle of the evening, Monsieur LaFlamme called a halt. Everyone gathered around the table to partake of the good things that the women had been preparing all afternoon—crepes suzettes with maple sugar, little cakes, fruit, and pots of coffee. André suggested a toast, and everyone raised their coffee to the eel that Michael had caught. André appeared with the eel washed and coiled neatly in a basket. The guests applauded and cheered for Michael. Monsieur LaFlamme motioned for him to take a bow.

"Get up, Michael, and say something," Merry whispered.

Michael got to his feet rather nervously and stammered his thanks. Quietness fell on the room as the guests turned toward him.

"I want to thank you for the kind hospitality you have shown to my sister and me," he began. "At school in England, we learned about Canada and your farming methods, but we never learned about how kind you are. So I say, 'Three cheers for the eel,' but even more, 'Three extra big cheers for the Ile d'Orleans and the LaFlamme family!' "

The guests cheered again and André shouted, "*Vive l'Angleterre!*"

"*Vive la Canada!*" Michael replied.

It was like a game as the cheers volleyed back and forth. Excitement mounted higher, and everyone started singing again. The fiddler took up his instrument, and soon the room twirled with dancers. When the bell in the church steeple struck midnight, the guests gathered their families together, wished each other well, and bade each other goodnight. As high-wheeled carriages rolled homeward over the straight, white roads, Michael and Merry climbed the stairs to their little rooms under the wide-sweeping roof.

Chapter 4

Ile d'Orleans

Rain was droning on the roof when Merry awoke the next morning. She lay still in bed, lulled by the sound. She slowly stretched her toes down to the foot of the bed. There was the soft patter of Madame LaFlamme's carpet slippers downstairs in the kitchen, the movement of a dish, the clatter of a pan on the stove. In the village, the church bell began its morning ringing. As the smell of breakfast began to waft through the house, Merry decided she could lie still no longer.

The conversation at breakfast was all about going to market that night. The earlier the start they got after supper, the better they would be able to display their wares to tempt the shrewd Quebec housewives and shopkeepers. The men and Michael pulled on long rubber boots and raincoats and headed outdoors to get the vegetables and the fish ready for market. The women of the household went to work at the loom which stood in a corner of the kitchen. There was a blanket to finish and a bedspread to begin. Wool, homespun and dyed in soft colors, lay in ready piles beside the loom.

"Ah, but you should be with us in the winter," Celeste said as she began working the treadle and the bright-colored wool moved into shape. "Then there are no outside tasks, and we work at the loom every day. My mother spins, my sister-in-law dyes, and I weave the wool into blankets and spreads and rugs.

"Where will they all be sold?" Merry asked.

"People will come from the city in the spring to buy them, and they will even go down into the United States."

The shuttle shot back and forth. Inches grew on the blanket as Celeste told of the deep winter when the thermometer dropped low and the snow piled high. Then none but the oxen or horses pulling sleighs could go along the roads. No one stirred from the village, and even the journey to church or to a friend's house was an adventure. The St. Lawrence River froze so solidly that horses with sleigh bells jingling in the crisp air could be driven across it. Merry thought of Mum and Daddy far away in London and wished that they and she and Michael could live in a little farmhouse with a sloping roof. She sat silently as Celeste worked.

"Your thoughts are far away," Celeste said, without looking up from her weaving.

"Oh—" Merry started. "Yes, they are."

"Despair and fear are riding the winds of the world these days, I think. They will find a place to lodge in our thoughts if we are not careful." Celeste looked up and smiled at Merry.

"You care for Britain, don't you, Celeste?"

"But of course," Celeste said quickly. "We may be French, but our loyalty to freedom is the same as yours. What we can do is small—raise food, weave woolens—but it all counts in the end." The movement of Celeste's hands stopped for a moment as she pointed to a thread. "Do you see that thread?"

Merry nodded.

"If it were weak, if it had a flaw, my blanket would be no good. It still might be nice to look at, but it would be of no use as a blanket. And the only problem would be one little thread."

Celeste began her work again, her hands moving swiftly back and forth. Threads interlocked, and the blanket grew— sky blue with bands of gold like the rich grain in the fields.

The rain of the morning cleared early, and the men busied themselves during the afternoon packing the cart with produce—potatoes, cabbages, carrots, onions. All were washed clean and tied in neat bunches. Michael laid apples in flat baskets. There was an armful of fresh cut flowers from Madame LaFlamme's garden, a box of fish, and the monster eel packed in a basket by himself.

After supper, Monsieur LaFlamme brought the oxen from the barn and hitched them to the cart. André clambered over the wheel and onto the driver's seat. Michael and Merry climbed up behind him. Among the bags of potatoes, Madame LaFlamme placed three of her warmest blankets.

"The children must have a place to rest," she said. "It will not be very comfortable, but it is better than no bed at all."

Soon they were off, the huge wheels of the cart moving slowly. Celeste held Pippin in her arms, and the women and children called goodbyes after the departing wagon. André sang to himself as they drove along, and the only other sounds were the soft pad of the oxen's hooves and the turning of the wheels.

As they drove, the sky changed from late twilight to darkest night. They crossed the long bridge with its span of lights necklaced out across the river. From the mainland, the Ile d'Orleans looked dark and distant. They now traveled on a road that had scarcely a turning until they reached the market square in Quebec. When they arrived, André slumped back in his seat and slept soundly.

In the north a fan of light spread up from the horizon into the dark sky. Merry caught her breath.

"Northern lights," Michael said in a low voice.

The lights seemed to be a flood of radiance, a gentle effusion that grew and decreased at the same time. It was silver white, then lemon yellow. The sky seemed to be filled with streamers. The light spread a pale glow over the cart and the oxen and the neat bunches of vegetables. There was a dreamy beauty to the night, and under its spell Merry felt stilled.

"I've been thinking about peace, Merry," Michael said.

Merry looked puzzled. "What about it?"

"Peace is the opposite of war, right?"

Merry nodded.

"Well, if war is destructive, then peace must be constructive. It's not just happiness and contentment—like life on this island. It's definitely progressive—so much so that at times it may even involve conflict."

"I see what you mean, Michael."

The last of the Northern lights faded from the sky, and they were encased again in starry darkness.

The next thing Michael and Merry knew it was daylight. A medley of voices filled the market square. There was little time to waste. It was five o'clock, and the people of Quebec came early to market. Michael and Merry purchased their breakfast at a nearby stall, and then they set to work helping André unload the produce and set it out on his stall.

The hours that followed were busy, for not a bunch of carrots could be sold without a conversation attached to it—admiration for the produce changed to dickering over the cost, then finally to pleased smiles all around as André pocketed the money and the carrots went off to flavor some soup pot. There were buyers from the hotels wanting to get the most for their money; nuns from the convents, their faces set off by stiff white collars, holding worn black purses; and mothers collecting a supply of fruits and vegetables and piling them all in small carts dragged by sleepy-eyed little children.

Merry weighed the fruit into baskets, and Michael wrapped up packages for people. André was often willing to turn a sale over to them, but they declined, knowing their

French would never stand the test of bargaining. The great moment of the day came when an offer was made for Michael's eel.

A large man, whom André seemed to know as a chef in one of the hotels in the upper part of town, stopped and looked at the eel. After watching transactions with Quebecois for the past three hours, Merry knew that his look of sleepy unconcern was only a mask for admiration. He leaned forward and pinched the eel as it lay coiled in its basket. André winked slyly at Michael.

"He is too big to be tender," the chef pronounced cryptically. "I will give you fifty cents for him."

"Three dollars," André said and turned back to his work of measuring out potatoes. The chef started to move away.

Michael started to speak, for fifty cents seemed quite sufficient for the eel, but André restrained him. Merry put her head down and pretended to be very busy inspecting a lettuce. She bit her lip to keep her laughter inside. The pompous chef and the pompous eel seemed to be a good match for each other.

The chef turned around. "Seventy-five cents," he offered grudgingly.

"Three dollars," André answered.

The chef turned and walked away.

"Why didn't you let him have it, André?" Michael asked. "That was a lot of money for an eel."

"Perhaps, but not for *that* eel. Besides, he will be back. I know when people have a mind to buy."

By now, more than half the produce they had started with had sold, and the rest was going rapidly as the crowds increased.

Twenty minutes later, the big chef could be seen pushing his way through the crowd back to the stall. He looked at the eel as if to assure himself that it was still there. Then he reached into his pocket and brought out two dollar bills which he placed in André's hand. He became all smiles as he tucked the basket with the eel under his arm and voiced admiration for its size.

André laughed and pulled Michael over to shake hands with the chef. Merry thought that they all could have been friends because they were so cheery with each other.

"But I thought you wanted three dollars for the eel," Michael said after the chef had left.

"Only so I could get two," André replied. With a grand gesture, he offered Michael one of the bills and was just as final about Michael's keeping it as he had been about the price.

When they reached the farmhouse later that night, everyone welcomed them as if they had been round the world. Madame LaFlamme was pleased to hear that one of the churches had bought her flowers to decorate their altar on Sunday, and Celeste was happy to receive orders for six blankets that would keep her loom busy for several weeks.

Then Madame LaFlamme remembered that a message had come from Uncle Tony in Quebec. Michael and Merry should be ready tomorrow morning, and he would call for them to go on their way to the United States.

"Oh!" Merry exclaimed, feeling like a pricked balloon. She was not ready to leave, not yet at least when there was such delight over a successful market day.

Uncle Tony arrived the next morning. One of his associates in Quebec had loaned him a car for the next week, Uncle Tony explained, so they could drive down to his friends in New Hampshire and he could then return to Quebec.

"Without us?" Michael asked.

Uncle Tony nodded.

Merry felt cold all over, and her voice sounded far away even to herself. "What are you going to do then, Uncle Tony?"

"Return to England," Uncle Tony said quietly. "My work here is done, for right now at least. I'm due back in London on the next boat."

They had only one more week with Uncle Tony, and then the Atlantic would be between them. He would be back near Mum and Daddy in a world at war. They would be alone.

She felt Michael's hand on her shoulder. She gave him a small smile when he patted her shoulder.

There was a great deal of noise and chatter as the suitcases were brought down and piled in the car. The whole LaFlamme family—Monsieur and Madame, André and Nicole, Celeste and Pierre, and all the children—kissed their English visitors on both cheeks and wished them well.

Uncle Tony started the engine. Slowly, the car pulled away from the clutter of children and chickens around the farmhouse gate and onto the straight road and across the bridge.

Chapter 5

Mountain Climbing

It was a long drive from Quebec to New Hampshire through a changing countryside. They crossed the border into the United States in the afternoon and arrived at Gorham in the evening. Uncle Tony thought it would be the best place to stop for the night since their eventual destination was still more than one hundred miles further south. Mountains hemmed the town, their dark bulks rising against the darkening sky. A small thrill of happiness went through Merry. It felt good to be around mountains again.

The next morning, sunlight flooded over the mountains, giving a warm radiance to one of the last days of September. Merry slipped out of bed and stood by the window watching the morning, thinking how the day seemed to belong to her especially. Then suddenly she remembered why. "It's my birthday today," she whispered to herself in surprise. The recent days had passed in such a strange new way that dates had been forgotten, and the twenty-fifth of September had arrived without any notice.

Merry remembered her previous birthdays spent in England with Mum and Daddy. When she awoke there, she would slip her hand under her pillow and discover some surprise. Last year it had been a small pin with one pearl that she wore on special occasions. Merry could even remember discovering a carved wooden horse one morning in the nursery when she was a little girl. Mum had always said that Merry herself had come at night, a rather special kind of present, so they had always put their presents for her under her pillow at night.

Merry dressed quickly, brushed her hair, and then hurried downstairs. Uncle Tony stood on the hotel porch, looking at the mountains. Merry joined him and slipped her hand into his.

"What does a mountain make you think of, Merry?"

Granite gleaming in the sun caught her eyes and held them. "What it would be like to stand on top," she answered.

Uncle Tony fell silent again. Merry nudged him a little.

"Uncle Tony, guess what day this is?"

"Wednes—" he began, then turned to look at her. Merry's eyes danced.

"Meredith Lamb!" he exclaimed. "It's your birthday!"

She laughed and nodded her head. Uncle Tony caught her in his arms and gave her such a big hug and kiss that it almost made up for missing Mum's and Daddy's. Then they sat together on the rail of the porch, their eyes drawn to the height of the mountain.

"Would a mountain be a good birthday present for you, Merry?"

"It would be the best ever! But what do you mean?"

"Well, we have the mountains and a few extra days and three sturdy mountaineers. Why shouldn't they all get together?"

"Why not?" Merry agreed with a smile.

Soon Michael and Pippin joined them on the porch. Michael placed a small package in Merry's hands.

"Happy birthday," he said with a smile and waited eagerly for her to open the present.

Merry's fingers undid the paper quickly. Inside she found a hand-woven scarf. The colors looked like a morning sky—pale pink and blue and yellow. The wool was soft and light to her touch.

"Celeste made it on her loom," Michael explained, "and the eel bought it."

"Oh, Michael, thank you!" Merry hugged him tightly. "Now I have something to wear when we go mountain climbing."

Michael's surprised eyes looked from Uncle Tony to Merry and back again. Merry laughed as Uncle Tony just smiled. On the way inside for breakfast, Merry told Michael about Uncle Tony's suggestion.

The dining room table displayed a real New England breakfast—baked apples followed by sausages and pancakes with a jug of amber-colored maple syrup from the sugar orchards of Vermont.

After breakfast, they brought out their mountain clothes—rucksacks, heavy boots, woolen socks, Merry's tough tweed skirt and Michael's shorts, pullovers, and leather jackets.

Uncle Tony spent the morning examining maps and telephoning the local guide for advice. At lunch he spread a map of the White Mountain National Forest on the table and pointed to Pinkham Notch with his pencil.

"We'll start here at the Appalachian Mountain Club Hut and take one of the trails up Mount Washington," he explained to Michael and Merry. "That will be a good morning's work. Then we can easily reach the Lakes of the Clouds Hut by afternoon to spend the second night there. If all goes well, we'll hike along the Presidential Range the next day and then swing back." Uncle Tony folded his map, and they sat down to eat their lunch.

It was late afternoon when they left Gorham and drove down the highway to Pinkham Notch. These mountains were different from any Michael and Merry had seen before. They looked rounder, cloaked in green forests. Dark pines blended with the gold of birches and the red flash of maples. In some places, the ranges came close together so the valley was in a shadow; elsewhere they veered apart and the flat land between gave space to farms and villages. Each village, no matter how small, had a white church with a fine tapering spire.

"If they were not wood and painted white, they might be the spires of London churches like St. Martin-in-the-Fields or St. Clement Danes," Merry said.

"They are called Christopher Wren spires after the ones in London that he designed," Uncle Tony explained, "so no wonder they look familiar to you."

The three travelers arrived at Pinkham Notch just before supper. They entered their names in the guestbook before going to their lodgings in one of the adjoining cabins. All the cabins were made of rough-hewn logs with fireplaces of field stone. They were sturdy and warm and comfortable.

Merry entered a small room with four bunks lining the walls. Each bunk had a mattress and pillow, several blankets, and a little green electric light. The light was designed to give enough light for one person to get to bed without waking other sleepers. Merry laid her rucksack on one of the beds and hurried over to the big cabin to meet Michael and Uncle Tony for supper.

There were about a dozen people gathered around the long trestle table. There were no formal introductions, but everyone chatted easily about the mountains and climbing. Uncle Tony said little and only asked questions that drew people to talk about themselves. Michael and Merry noticed that since he had been working for the government he had been far less talkative than ever before.

"Have you done much climbing?" a young man asked Merry, passing her a tin plate of beans.

"Not too much," she said. "Just a bit with my uncle and brother in Switzerland and Iceland."

His eyes widened in admiration. "That's just that many more places in the world than I've ever been to," he exclaimed.

After dinner, the climbers relaxed around the fire with its blazing logs. Some of the climbers brought out maps and showed the trails they had done or hoped to do while others compared mountain experiences. Uncle Tony asked for a good trail up Mount Washington that they might take the next morning. The climbers suggested several, some for the view and others for the time. A seasoned climber recommended Lion Head, and Uncle Tony began charting it on his map. A few hours later, the climbers headed to their cabins. Goodnights echoed through the cold air.

The big gong hanging outside the main cabin sounded at 6:45 A.M. Dressing did not take long as many had slept in their clothing, and by seven o'clock the crowd of the night before had gathered around the breakfast table. They ate quickly since most of the climbers were eager to be off on the trails inside of an hour. Breakfast was a noble affair, and the dishes down the table were piled with stewed apricots, oatmeal, eggs, bacon, corn bread, juice, milk, and coffee.

The sky was gray and overcast, but it altered no one's plans since weather in the valley was no indication of weather on the summit. Above timber it might be sunny or stormy, and there was an equal chance of either. The cool wind that was blowing held the warning of winter. Merry knotted her birthday scarf comfortably around her neck. She and Michael waved to some of the climbers heading off up a trail. Uncle Tony joined them and handed them their lunches. They packed the paper bags into their rucksacks, then pulled the rucksacks onto their backs. After saying goodbye to Pippin, who would stay with the hut keeper, the three mountain climbers headed up the wide Lion Head Trail that rose immediately and narrowed quickly as the other trails branched away from it.

Trees with thinning leaves arched overhead as they hiked. Sometimes the path went beside an old stone wall, the broken remains of a land boundary. For a while, a chipmunk raced along the wall beside them. Michael broke some bits from a chocolate bar and tossed them to the chipmunk. Further on they discovered deer tracks although the deer themselves seemed to be in hiding.

The path slowly narrowed and grew rockier. They stopped to catch their breath and saw the low gray ceiling of clouds resting far down the mountains. They crossed a stream that foamed and splashed over granite boulders. When they reached a clearing in the woods, they stopped to look at the ascent before them. A formation of boulders stood out sharply against the heavy gray of the sky. Merry could discern a rough but realistic-looking lion's head with a large jaw and alert ears. The lion's profile reminded Michael of the four bronze lions in Trafalgar Square in London.

"I'll bet you don't know why they never put the British lion on a postage stamp, Uncle Tony," Michael asked.

"I certainly don't," Uncle Tony answered.

"Because he won't be licked."

Uncle Tony nodded with a grin. "Nor will we. Come on, let's get going."

The trail soon began to close in so that it was scarcely visible. It rose so steeply that it looked like a stairway of earth and rock and twisted tree roots.

"Don't follow too close," Uncle Tony warned, "and test your holds before you trust them." He led the way, his hands and feet finding niches in the rocks. Michael held back to give Uncle Tony some distance, then Merry waited for Michael to lead off. It was hard but exhilarating work, like mounting a ladder of giant steps. Merry felt as if her breath came from her toes. Her muscles tightened as her fingers and feet sought their holds.

Above her, Uncle Tony and Michael had reached a level place in the trail. Merry turned her head slightly and looked down into the valley below. There was nothing but treetops and the downward surge of space. She closed her eyes as a sickening feeling swept over her. All the nerve she had ever had seemed to be oozing out of her. Fighting for breath, she realized that she would have to tell Uncle Tony and Michael to go on over the Lion Head Trail without her. She would take Boott Spur and meet them at the top of the mountain. She started to look down once more, but another wave of fear made her stop.

"No," she muttered, her face pressing against the granite slab. "No, I won't look down." She clenched her jaw and tightened her grip on the rock.

"Coming, Merry?" Uncle Tony's voice sounded far above her.

"Yes, I—I'm coming," she called.

"Need a hand?" Michael asked.

"No, I'm fine." She looked up the length of rock toward them. There was a place for her fingers and another for her knee. She grasped the rock with both hands and found in relief that she had the entire mountain to support her.

When she reached the top of the rock, she found Michael waiting for her. Uncle Tony had gone on ahead.

"Michael, was I awfully long down there?"

"No, of course not. But don't bother to look down at the view, Merry, until we get to the top. It's always much better from up there."

"I won't," she promised quickly.

They continued on until they reached a white sign with green lettering.

White Mountain National Forest
If the weather is bad, you are advised to turn back
and make the ascent at a more favorable time. The
route to the summits is treacherous in stormy and
foggy weather. Follow the markers closely.

"How awful it must be to get turned back," Michael commented.

The timber shortly came to an abrupt end, and they found themselves in a high open world, a wild bare plateau of moss and rocks a thousand feet below the summit. The wind blew strongly, and the sky was thick with fast-moving clouds.

Uncle Tony found a shelter from the wind behind some boulders and called to Michael and Merry to follow him. They pulled their paper bags out of their rucksacks and settled down to eat their lunch. In each bag were several sandwiches wrapped neatly in wax paper, a bag of raisins, and a bar of chocolate.

It was nearly noon, and the sky was still gray with low clouds. Mount Washington was the highest peak in the northeast, and on a clear day, climbers could see the Atlantic Ocean on one side and the Adirondack Mountains on the other. But today there would be no such view.

Michael and Merry and Uncle Tony continued on after their lunch. They found several notices posted along the trail warning climbers to turn back if weather conditions were dangerous. Merry stopped to read one aloud.

To Climbers Above Timberline
Weather conditions in the mountains are subject to
sudden and severe changes. Hut masters are in-
structed to give you the benefit of their opinion and to
exercise cautious judgment, but the Club does not as-

sume responsibility for the accuracy of any weather predictions.

"We don't have to turn back, do we?" Michael asked.

"Oh, no," Uncle Tony answered. "The weather isn't bad, not yet anyway. We'll have to stay alert, but we can certainly go on."

They pushed on over the granite boulders. Further on, several trails converged at a spring bubbling under the rocks. They each took a drink of icy mountain water, then continued up to the summit over sharp stones and massive rocks. The higher they climbed, the harder it was to see. Breathing hard and warm from exertion, they now had no more than a hundred feet to do.

Then suddenly they were there on the rocky summit of Mount Washington. Instead of seeing hundreds of miles, they saw perhaps ten feet. They could make out the dim outline of the weather station and the nearer outline of the Summit House looming before them.

Inside the Summit House, Michael and Merry warmed themselves before the fire while Uncle Tony talked with one of the attendants. They left their rucksacks on their backs since they would be leaving soon to go down the mountain a short way to the hut where they would spend the night. Uncle Tony soon joined them by the fire.

"What did he say, Uncle Tony?" Merry asked.

"The winds are expected to reach gale force, but they should shift to the north soon which will clear the clouds out. Well, we'd better get going if we expect to reach the hut before darkness."

They started off again into the wind-swirled mist. The way was not hard as most of it was downhill. They walked quickly, trying to race against the wind and the ever-darkening clouds. They passed two small lakes—the Lakes of the

Clouds—whose black water was whipped into agitated waves by the wind.

Just ahead they spotted a small but snug and welcoming hut. It was built of stone and locked to the mountain.

Chapter 6

A Night on the Mountain

A young man cheerfully welcomed Uncle Tony, Michael, and Merry when they reached the hut. He led them to their bunks—Michael's and Tony's in the men's dormitory and Merry's across the hall in the women's dormitory. The bunk beds rose from the floor to the ceiling, and the rooms were able to accommodate crowds of people. Each thin mattress had a blue checked pillow and a pile of gray blankets. They placed their rucksacks and jackets on their bunks before following the hut master into the kitchen.

The tin stove held a crackling, warm fire. Dishes and supplies filled the shelves above the stove, and two tables with long benches sat in the center of the room. The three weary travelers sat down at the table, and the hut master soon placed steaming cups of tea before them.

"I'm Bill Everett," he introduced himself as he joined them at the table. "My brother Bob and I are the only ones up here right now—he's bringing supplies down from the summit and should be back soon. All the other climbers have returned to town. There aren't many climbers on the range this late in the season."

Bill and Bob were in college, and they and four other helpers spent their summers taking care of the hut. They cooked and cleaned, guided the climbers along the trails, and kept the hut stocked with supplies. When the huts closed in a week, they would return to their college work in the cities.

"We can usually make the football team without too much trouble," Bill told them with a laugh. "Here comes Bob now," he said.

A young man cheerfully welcomed Uncle Tony, Michael, and Merry when they reached the hut.

Michael and Merry looked toward the window where he was pointing. They could see a man swiftly running down the slope with a large pack on his back. He soon reached the hut and deposited his load on the kitchen floor. There were long pieces of wood, a tin of fuel oil, and a crate of supplies.

"It's rough up at the summit," Bob told them after Bill made the introductions. "I hope there aren't many people on the mountain tonight."

"Did you come over Washington today or one of the lower trails?" Bill asked Uncle Tony.

"Washington, and we looked for that famous view we've read so much about, but we couldn't see anything except our hands in front of our faces."

"That's what it's like to live in the clouds," Bill said. "We get all kinds of weather up here, mostly bad this time of year."

"How did you come up the mountain?" Bob asked.

"Over Lion Head," Uncle Tony answered.

"Lion Head!" both Bob and Bill exclaimed in admiration. "That's the stiffest way up Washington," Bob told them. "There's only one better, Huntington Ravine."

Bob hung a lantern in the window to guide any late travelers to the hut. Merry peered out the window, but with the oncoming twilight and the swirling clouds pressing about the hut, there was little to be seen. Her eyes narrowed as she saw movement.

"I think someone's coming," she called to Bob. "Alone too."

When the others joined her at the window, they could discern a girl stumbling along, leaning her body against the wind. Her shoulder length hair was flying straight out in the wild rush of wind. Finally she arrived at the hut and followed Bob into the kitchen. Her cheeks were red from the wind, and she was breathing deeply.

"Have you come far?" Bill asked, pouring out some tea for her.

She nodded.

"You're going to stay the night, aren't you?"

"No, no, I must get back to the base station tonight," she answered. Her voice was rich and throaty. "My name is Julie," she added. She looked slowly around the room, fixing her cool gray eyes on everyone in turn as they introduced themselves. She was a few years older than Merry and Michael, and when she spoke, words rolled off her tongue in a foreign way.

"I shall go down the Ammonoosuc Ravine. It is faster that way, yes?"

Bill laughed uneasily. "You won't go down tonight if I have anything to say about it."

Julie tossed her wind-swept hair and jingled a bracelet on her wrist. Little charms were attached to it—one of them was a small mouth organ. She shrugged her shoulders at Bill and began to play a little tune on her mouth organ. Grieg's "Ich Liebe Dich" filled the room. Merry hummed the tune she had learned as a child.

"Is she German?" Michael whispered to Uncle Tony.

Uncle Tony shook his head.

When the notes died away, Uncle Tony turned toward Julie. "Did you get your mouth organ in Austria?" he asked.

"In Vienna where I used to live," she said with a nod. "Where I am going back to someday." She turned and looked at Bill. "Who are you to tell me what I should do?" she asked. "I have done more real climbing in one summer than you have done all your life."

"No doubt you have," Bill agreed good-naturedly.

"And on real mountains too, not just these piles of stones you call mountains. I like a mountain to be dangerous." Julie's eyes flashed. "There is no danger here."

"The weather—"

"Poof! A little mist, a little wind—that is nothing." She shrugged her shoulders and started playing the little mouth organ again.

Merry's usually pleasant nature began to darken. She turned to chat with Michael in an attempt to dismiss Julie from her mind.

A little while later Bob and Bill combined their efforts to make supper. Two other climbers arrived, one yodeling from a great distance to announce their coming.

It was a strange group that gathered around the table that evening to an even stranger meal. There was some sort of rice and beans dish along with fruit and tea. As a special treat, Bob had mixed up an impressive looking spice cake. There were rather a lot of raisins in the mahogany-colored batter that tasted mainly of nutmeg and cinnamon.

The cake was far from appreciated. After a few mouthfuls, the consensus of opinion was that Bob had been so long surrounded by granite rocks that they had somehow got into his cooking. Merry did her best to finish her piece, but Bill wanted to throw the cake away.

"No," Bob said firmly, "we'll find some use to put it to."

The group around the table laughed, and one of the newcomers threatened instant retaliation if the spice cake ever made a second appearance.

The edge of ice that had started to form earlier in the evening began to thaw slowly. Julie was amusing, if somewhat irritating, as she told of her mountain climbs in Austria. Snow like Austria's never fell anywhere else, nor was there any place in the world where the sun shone so brightly and the people were so cheerful. Julie was relatively safe from argument since no one in the group except for Uncle Tony had ever been to Austria, and he said nothing.

Sam and Carl, the recent arrivals, were an odd pair. Carl was strong and husky, came from the Midwest, and was heading back there for college. Sam was pale and earnest. He worked in a city but came to the mountains for his holidays. The two young men had met on the trail and joined up together. Carl's clothes were casual, tossed together and battered. Sam's clothes looked new, his boots were polished, and his jacket was unstained. He looked like an advertisement for "what the well-dressed mountaineer should wear"—and what the real one never does.

Carl claimed to have climbed every mountain in the East. Sam had been near the summit of many mountains but had never actually made it, for something always happened that cut his holiday and his achievement short. Merry imagined that he must be in love with a girl who had said she would marry him if he would climb to the top of just one mountain, but his nerve always failed him and there was always a convenient excuse.

"It doesn't look as if I'll make Washington this time since the weather is so uncertain," Sam said. Merry bit her lip to keep from laughing.

Everyone helped to clear the table, wash the dishes, and tidy the kitchen. Then the group pulled their benches and chairs around the stove, and Julie played her mouth organ while the rest joined in singing. After a while, Bob and Bill began to tell stories about rescues made from the hut.

"One night about a year ago," Bob began, "two climbers staying with us insisted on going their way even against warning. It had rained all that day, and when they left the hut the temperature was dropping rapidly. Ice forms dangerously on the rocks in that kind of weather, and an hour later some of the others in the hut thought they heard distress calls—three sharply repeated sounds. So we formed a search party.

"It was hard going," Bob went on, "because the rocks were covered in ice, and the wind made some of the ice fly through the air."

"Did you find them?" Michael asked.

"We did, but we nearly lost a man over the ravine doing it."

Bill then told a story of three climbers who were determined to take a certain dangerous trail down from the summit. They were missing for three days on the mountains, and every ranger, woodsman, guide, and hut man for miles around came to search for them. The search party found the men alive, but the mountain people felt that such luck was undeserved because the climbers had stubbornly disregarded every warning.

"These are the good stories," Bill commented. "There are plenty of others that are not so good. Not long ago, three students who had never climbed before thought they would come to the mountains for a holiday. They didn't have any proper equipment, and their clothing was far from suitable. One afternoon they left the hut where they had eaten lunch in order to try to reach another hut by nightfall. Before long, one of the boys gave out. It was getting dark, and the weather was getting bad. His friends left him to try to get help. When they reached the hut, the hut men went back to search for the friend. There's a cross there now where he went to sleep."

"There's an old rule that's true everywhere," Uncle Tony said, "that mountains are only safe for those who respect them."

"Exactly," Bill agreed, "whether they're six thousand feet or twenty-six thousand."

"These mountains have claimed a few lives," Bob said, "but there hasn't been one accident that we've known of where it could have been prevented if the climbers had heeded advice or used real mountain skill."

Outside, the wind was moaning and battering the hut. Julie put her mouth organ to her lips and started to drown out the wail of the wind. She played one well-known song after another, nodding to the group to encourage them to sing. But the wood was getting low, and the fire could not be stoked indefinitely. One by one the climbers began to head to their bunks.

"See you at breakfast," Bob called to Julie when she rose to leave.

"Perhaps, and perhaps not," she replied. "If I feel like going earlier, I shall do so."

"There's not much chance of the weather changing in the next twelve hours," Bill reminded her. "Better plan to relax up here tomorrow. Nothing is worth the risk of getting into trouble on the mountain."

Julie tossed her head. "Who are you to tell me what to do?" She left the room and headed to the women's dormitory.

Bill looked helplessly at Uncle Tony. "A hut man's suggestions are supposed to be law up here, but what can you say against that?"

"Can't you just say, 'Nobody leaves the hut without my permission'?" Michael asked.

"No, I can't. I'm not a policeman. People are supposed to respond, but if they don't—well, that's all there is to it."

They all left the room after saying goodnight. Merry lighted her way into the dormitory with her small pocket flashlight and found her bunk. She pulled off her heavy boots and folded her pullover over the pillow to act as a cover, then slipped between the gray blankets.

The wind roared outside, battling against the windows, shaking the hut until it trembled. Pitiful and sad sounds filled the room. Merry lay wide-awake. She thought of London and her bedroom and Mum, and she wished she could be there. Instead she was in a hut on a high mountain with a not-so-friendly girl for company. She would have liked to talk to Julie, but she felt unsure as to how Julie would respond. Merry raised her head from the pillow.

"Goodnight, Julie," she whispered softly.

There was no answer for a long moment, then three small saucy notes played on the tiny mouth organ filled the black silence of the room. Merry put her head back down on the pillow, feeling a strange desire to cry.

The wind roared on, and the hut shook like a ship weathering a fierce gale. The wind whipped around the corners, finding small chinks to enter and filling the hut with the northern cold. Sleeping figures blanketed in gray rolls lay still in their dormitories. In the kitchen, the fire had long since gone out. Sometimes a door banged or a window creaked, but nothing could be heard above the crescendo of the wind.

Toward morning the wind dropped, and the blackness of night thinned into gray. One of the sleepers stirred. A blanket unrolled and a shivering figure stood up, pulled on outdoor clothing, and laced up boots. The figure crept silently over the floor and to the door. The falling swish of the wind covered all noises. The figure stood for a moment on the threshold of the open door, then slipped out into the predawn grayness.

An hour later, the morning had more light but not more warmth. The wind rose again in an angry force. Mist came along with the rain, blotting out the impress of nailed boots on the trail leading down to the Ammonoosuc Ravine.

Chapter 7

Missing!

When Merry awoke, morning light had filled the room. She could hear the wind still blowing wildly outside the hut. Icy rain beat on the windows. Merry lay still, shivering at the thought of leaping out of her warm blankets into the chilly room. But then she heard plates clattering in the kitchen and smelled coffee and frying bacon. That was enough to make her push the blankets back. The room was frigid, so she quickly slid her pullover over her head and laced her boots. She glanced toward Julie's bunk, relieved to see a long, straight roll of blanket. Since Julie seemed to be still asleep, there might be some peace at breakfast.

Merry entered the kitchen and found the others getting ready to sit down to breakfast.

"Where's the harmonica player?" Bob asked.

"She's still asleep," Merry answered, sitting down at the table beside Uncle Tony. "She was all wound up in her blankets. Do you want me to call her?"

"No, that's okay," Bill said with a smile. "Let her sleep in comfort, and let us eat in peace."

"I'm glad she didn't make off in the night," Bob said. He set a dish of stewed apricots on the table. "Some people always want to go their own way. I thought she might give us some trouble, but it looks as if I was wrong."

The kitchen was warm, and everyone was cheerful in spite of the fact that they were stranded in the hut for another day. There were jobs to do around the hut, books to read, and letters to write. The day would pass quietly and enjoyably.

It was after ten o'clock when they had the table cleared and the dishes washed and dried. They had just pulled the benches up around the tin stove to settle down to the morning when there was a knock on the kitchen door. Bob opened the door, and two young men staggered in, the nails on their boots ringing on the floor. They sank down in exhaustion on a bench near the fire. They were dripping wet, and their hair was plastered to their heads. Putting down little cardboard lunch boxes that were soaked through with rain, they held out their stiff hands to the stove's heat.

Bill spoke first. "Where have you come from?"

"The base station. We work there at the hotel," the older boy answered.

"You didn't choose much of a day for your trip," Bob commented.

The younger boy smiled grimly. "Doesn't seem so here, but it was a grand day down at the base. The sun was shining. We've been looking at the peak all summer, and this was our only chance to climb Washington. We're supposed to head back to town tomorrow."

"Was it rough going, boys?" Bill asked as the two young men drew closer to the warmth and pulled off their coats and sodden boots.

"Nothing at all until we got above the timberline," the younger boy said. "Then it was like a different world, so much rain and wind. But we thought we'd keep on, thought it might get better. It got worse."

"Why didn't you go back?" Sam asked.

"We tried to, but we couldn't see the path or the markers."

"How did you find the hut?"

The boys looked at each other. "Don't know. We just looked up, and there it was."

"You mean you weren't even heading for the hut?"

"No, we were heading for Washington."

Bill whistled. "It's your lucky day all right. We're the only hut for miles around. You wouldn't have held out much longer, and we wouldn't have even known anyone was lost on the mountain."

"We still want to get to the top," the elder boy said.

Bill shook his head. "I can't let you, boys. No one leaves the hut today. It's not safe."

"But we have to go back to town tomorrow."

"Well, at least you'll go back alive," Bill said. He scooped up the two limp and miserable-looking lunch boxes and tossed them into the fire. "Go on into the men's dormitory and rest, and take all the blankets you want. I'll call you when it's time for lunch. A good hot meal will make you think there's still a lot to live for."

The two boys shuffled out of the room.

"How much longer do you think they could have held out?" Carl asked.

"Not many minutes," Bob replied. "They were nearly ready to collapse when they came in. First thing they would have done outdoors would have been to sit down on a rock for a rest, and the next thing the cold would've gotten them."

Bill sighed. "Well, all's well that ends well. As long as the food and fuel hold out, we should all be happy."

"What do you suppose Julie is doing?" Uncle Tony asked. "She can't be sleeping all this time!"

"The beds are too uncomfortable for that!" Sam laughed.

"I'll go and call her," Merry offered, slipping out of the warm room and into the cold dormitory.

Julie's bunk looked just as it had earlier, the blankets wound in a long roll and pulled up a little around the pillow. Merry hesitated a moment, then she reached out her hand to gently shake Julie. As Merry touched the blanket, her breath caught in a small gasp. Julie was not under the blankets. Merry's mind raced back to the early morning. She could not remember actually seeing Julie. She had only glanced quickly at Julie's bunk before hurrying out to the warm kitchen. A cold feeling crept over Merry. She shivered and fled back to the kitchen.

"Julie's not there!" she cried. The babble of voices in the room ceased. All eyes fastened on Merry, and no one spoke for a long minute.

"When did she leave?" Bill asked, breaking the silence.

"It must have been before I got up." Merry blurted out the whole appalling truth. "I thought she was still asleep—the blankets—everything." Merry slowly sat down.

Bill looked at her. "Don't worry. It wasn't your fault if you thought she was asleep." He left the room and could be heard rummaging in the neighboring dormitory. He came back into the kitchen holding an envelope in his hand. "She's left some money for her supper and lodging, but otherwise she's gone every bit and all belongings. Must have slipped out early this morning. Independent lass, isn't she?"

"When she first arrived, she said she wanted to go down by the Ammonoosuc Ravine," Michael put in.

"Ammonoosuc," Bill repeated. "Well, there's a chance she might have made it even in the mist if she got off the rocks and into timber before the rain came. I should find a telephone to see if she made it. If she didn't, we'll have to get a squad out."

"The nearest telephone is at the summit," Bob reminded him.

"Yes, and it's a job and a half to get to it, but we'll have to do it. I'll take someone with me; one alone out on the mountain isn't much good in this weather. Bob, you take charge here. No one goes out. Keep a sharp lookout. If the wind drops, listen for distress calls." His eyes swept across the group, disqualifying people at a glance.

Uncle Tony stepped forward. "I'd be glad to go with you."

Bill shook his head. "Thanks, but I'll need you when we get back. I don't believe she made it, so I'll need a strong rescue team." His gaze lighted on Michael.

Michael rose as if he'd been called to attention. "I'd be glad to go," he said.

Bill turned to Uncle Tony. "Has he done much climbing—rough work, I mean?"

Uncle Tony nodded. "He's done a bit. He can keep his feet under him."

"When do we start?" Michael asked eagerly.

"Instantly. Too much time has been lost already."

Merry smiled at her brother as he pulled on his coat, glad that he would help to correct something that seemed to be her fault.

Michael stood almost as tall as Bill, though not so broad, and the two looked fit for anything as they started out. Merry ran to the window and pressed her face to the glass, eager to watch them up the summit. But they had scarcely gone ten paces from the hut when the swirling mist and rain had obliterated all trace of them.

"When will they be back?"

"It's nearly an hour's trip one way in good weather," Bob answered as he started to prepare lunch.

While the others turned to different tasks or amusements, Merry felt like a prisoner of the howling wind. The hut seemed almost unbearably small. Uncle Tony smiled at her, seeming to sense that she needed something to do.

"Have you folded up the blankets in the dormitory yet?" he asked her.

Merry shook her head.

"Well, that's one job for us. I expect there are a few things we might find to do together that will save Bill some work when he gets back."

Merry nodded and followed Uncle Tony out of the kitchen.

"I wish we could do more, Uncle Tony!"

"I feel the same way. But no one knows what may come about before the day's over or what we may be called on to do."

Merry smiled at her uncle as she held up another blanket for them to fold.

Bill and Michael found the going no worse and no better than they had expected to find it. The wind was strong against them, but it often kept them from falling because the rocks were slippery with rain and the moss patches were spongy. The mist had closed in so that midday seemed like twilight, and the rain drove hard.

They were able to stay on a safe path by following the cairns, markers formed by rough piles of granite slabs topped with white. Bill set a fast pace up the steep incline since he was used to packing loads up and down the mountains, but Michael was in good condition and kept up with him. They stopped just short of the summit for a rest. They could hear the wind instruments on the weather station spinning wildly, but they could see nothing. Bill looked at his watch.

"How long?" Michael asked, breathing deeply.

"Fifty minutes," Bill said proudly. "That's sharp going in good weather."

"Much more?" Michael could speak only in monosyllables.

"A few more steps, but the wind will be worse. Ready?"

Michael nodded.

They pushed on. The wind was worse, coming at them from all sides. Michael fought against it but could not help being swayed off his track. Soon the outline of the weather station appeared before them. They gripped the walls for support as they made their way to the door.

The radio man was at his post. He turned quickly, staring at them as if they were apparitions.

Bill laughed. "What's the wind?"

"Eighty miles," the man replied, "with blasts of a hundred. I've just clocked it. But what are you doing out in it?"

"Just came up to the summit to make a telephone call."

The man whistled. "I wouldn't think anything could be that important! Is everything all right at the hut?"

Bill nodded. "We've got an appointment with a girl and have to see if she's keeping it."

"Must be some girl," the man said, then turned away as the radio began buzzing.

Bill called goodbye, and he and Michael left to tackle the wind for the small space between the weather station and the Summit House.

Michael warmed himself by the fire while Bill made the telephone call. When Bill returned, Michael could tell what Bill was going to say by the way he walked across the room.

"No one has come into the base station all day," Bill began. "She was expected. She was supposed to meet a group of college girls who have had to go on without her. So," he said, buttoning up his coat, "she's on the mountain, and we're responsible for her."

They headed out again into the wind. Michael quickly saw that a different technique was required for going down the trail. Watching the rock ahead and placing one foot where the eye thought it should go was not enough. Michael soon learned to make allowance for wind drift and place his foot further to one side. Bill did not want to lose another minute, so his pace was even quicker than before. They ran where the rocks allowed it, following the guidance of the cairns.

The people left in the hut had just finished their lunch when Bill and Michael came plunging in. They told the news quickly, its grim importance dawning on the listeners. It was like a mystery with no clues, for Julie might be fifty feet or five miles from the hut. There was no possible way of telling.

Bill organized his search party quickly. Every able climber in the hut had some job to do, some responsibility. Michael and Merry were given charge of the hut. The two young men who had arrived that morning glanced hopefully at Bill, but Bill sent them back to the dormitory for more rest. They still looked pale and dazed. At the brief request, they turned willingly and went back to their bunks.

Bill had a few last-minute instructions for Merry and Michael. "The hut must never be left without someone in it. It stands here as a refuge and no one knows when it may be needed."

The rescue team made up of Bill, Bob, Sam, Carl, and Uncle Tony filed out of the hut. Uncle Tony turned and smiled at Michael and Merry. Then they were gone with their ropes, staves, flares, and emergency kit. The mist and the wind swallowed them up.

Chapter 8

Rescue

Michael went off to a corner of the room to write in his travel journal, which he had been keeping since they had left England. He was some days behind and knew that he could use an hour or so to catch up.

Merry searched the supply shelves, wondering if she might start something for supper in case it was late when the rescuers got back. She had never done much cooking, but the little she had done had left a small store that she called upon now. She found Bob's disaster of a spice cake near the back of the top shelf.

"Michael," she said, "I'm going to make a surprise for everyone. Will you promise not to look around until I say you can?"

"Certainly," Michael said without raising his head.

The cake was still in the tin and had hardly a dent in it since so few pieces had been cut the night before. It was hard as a rock. Looking at it, Merry's idea gradually took form. She found the meat grinder in a drawer and, putting the cake through it, soon had a bowl of brownish crumbs streaked through with the dark of raisins. She beat up two eggs and mixed them with the crumbs, then added a cup of warm milk. The mixture looked like any ordinary cake batter, but a taste still told tellingly of spice.

Merry thought for a moment, wondering how to counter the flavor. Then she pulled a packet of shelled walnuts and a bar of bitter chocolate from the cupboard. She put them through the grinder and added them to the batter. She tasted it again. The batter now had a delicious chocolate flavor with a background of something indefinable, which Daddy said was the mark of a good cook. Merry poured the mixture into a deep baking dish. She would bake it for half an hour or so before dinner and serve it hot with a creamy sauce.

With such an accomplishment behind her, Merry felt full of energy and annoyingly idle. She went over and sat near Michael, who was still busily writing.

"When do you think they'll be back?"

"Don't know. When they find her."

"Rotten business, isn't it? I can't believe Julie's putting everyone to all this trouble."

Michael scribbled a few more words before closing his book and putting it in his pocket. He knew Merry would persist in talking even if he tried to keep writing.

"Do you think Julie is a spy?" Merry asked in a hushed voice.

Michael stared at Merry, his eyes filled with amazement. "Why, Meredith Lamb, whatever makes you think such things?"

"Oh, the way she speaks for one thing; the horrid way she looks at people for another. Under cover of mist, she might be spying out all sorts of things on the top of these mountains."

Michael was about to laugh, but, thinking of the radio station on the summit, he began to see some possibility of logic in her allegation. However, he shook his head slowly.

"I hardly think she could be. She wouldn't be quite so clumsy if she were."

"I hate people like that," Merry said bitterly.

"Why?" Michael asked. He found it hard to follow Merry's reasoning.

"Because—" Merry stopped. She had thought a whole tirade of words was on the tip of her tongue, but now there seemed to be nothing there. There really wasn't any reason she should dislike Julie except that they did not understand each other. Merry felt oddly deflated. "Oh, just because I do," she answered lamely.

"That's not a very good reason to hate someone," Michael said.

Suddenly Merry felt as if she were back in London with Daddy sitting on the edge of her bed in the early hours of that last morning. She remembered Daddy's request that she never allow herself to hate anything or anybody no matter what happened. Merry heard her own voice answering, "I promise, Daddy."

Yet here she was, in peace and safety on a mountaintop, with hate burning in her heart.

"I've broken my promise to Daddy," Merry said. She told Michael everything, from the early morning promise to the way Julie refused to say goodnight in the dormitory.

"You can always make your promise again, Merry. You can start over and strive not to break it again."

Merry smiled at her brother. "You're right." Merry felt a new determination to help Julie in any way she could.

A few minutes later, the door opened, and the two boys who had been sleeping came into the kitchen. They looked much more refreshed than they had earlier.

"It looks as if the weather is clearing up a bit," one of them said.

Merry looked out the window. Neither she nor Michael had been thinking about the weather for the past hour, so the change came as a complete surprise. Light was now streaking through the heavy mists, and the wind was blowing more gently.

Michael went to the door and opened it. A rift in the clouds revealed the whole downward slope of the mountain and the valley far below. The river threading through the valley caught the sun's rays and looked like a golden ribbon bound about a brilliantly green world. Merry took a deep breath of the fresh damp air.

"Michael, we've been in the hut all day. We should go out for a walk."

"I don't think we should, Merry," Michael said. "At least not until the others get back."

The elder of the two boys stepped forward. "We'd be glad to take charge of the hut if you and your sister would like to go out for a few minutes."

"It would be fine, Michael," Merry urged. "We could just take a quick walk in front of the hut."

Michael looked at the boys, now fit and alert. Merry's idea seemed sensible as long as they did not go too far.

"All right," Michael said, "but we can't go far in case the others come back."

While Merry went to collect their coats, Michael and the boys agreed that Michael would give a shout every five minutes that the boys would answer so that Merry and Michael could keep close to the hut and find their way back in case the mist closed over again.

They stood in the doorway of the hut for a moment, filling their lungs with the cold, clean mountain air. Sometimes a finger of light pierced the clouds, making the rocks shine like massive diamonds. Sometimes the wind dropped so completely that there was a space of silence broken only by the rushing of the mountain streams.

Michael and Merry started up the trail in silence. Low bushes with glistening leaves and huge wet rocks interspersed with mossy places bordered the trail. They tried to find tracks that would indicate which way the searchers had taken, but the rain had blotted out every sign. They stood still and listened to the music of the little streams that were tumbling down to the valley. Sometimes they sounded like the rippling chimes of a clock, sometimes like the long lilt of a violin. Then the sounds ceased, but the water kept running and the sound was just that and no more—a brook slipping over sizeable stones.

Michael and Merry looked at each other in amazement.

"How strange," Merry said. "It must be an echo."

The wind came whipping around them again, taking away all sounds in its low moan. When it died down, Michael let out his voice for the five-minute shout and received almost instantly an answering shout from the hut. Just then the curious tinkling sound started up again.

"It's music," Merry said slowly.

"Probably made by the wind, the water, or even the mountains," Michael answered.

"No, I don't think so," Merry said, laying her hand on his sleeve to silence him. "Real music. Listen."

And then, faintly, came the tune "Ich Liebe Dich."

Michael strained his ears to catch the direction, then looked at Merry. "It must be Julie."

"It can't be anything else but her little mouth organ," Merry whispered.

The sound was so faint, so wispily carried about by the wind, and then it ceased altogether. Michael shouted again, but it brought forth no other sound than the shout from the hut already agreed upon.

"It was over there, wasn't it, Merry?" Michael pointed east and up the mountain.

"I thought it was over there." She pointed west and down the mountain.

"Well, it couldn't have been more than a hundred feet away, or we would never have heard it between the wind's gusts. Let's start on the west and cover the ground in an arc to the east."

They made a pile of stones to mark the place at which they were starting. Foot by foot they traversed ground, looking for tracks or any trace, listening intently to catch the faintest sound.

"We're coming, Julie, but where are you?" Merry called out to the mountain stillness.

There was a faint answering sound. It might have been the wind caught in one of the rock crannies. If it was the curious music, it was nearer. They kept calling as they searched, but heard no other answer. Merry kept repeating to herself the sentence Daddy had taught her in London. "It all depends on me, and I depend on God."

The sky was now clear, but twilight darkened the sky. The boys at the hut had already hung a lantern in the window, and its assuring light streamed out over the rocks. Michael and Merry had come without their flashlights and soon would be forced back to the hut. Stumbling over the stones in the increasing darkness, they kept calling out at intervals.

"Here's her scarf," Michael cried out triumphantly as he picked up a bright silk square, bedraggled but still recognizable.

"Michael!" Merry exclaimed. He turned to look where she was pointing. There was Julie, very limp and very still, in a hollow under a rock. Her eyes were closed. Her face was pale. Her torn and bruised hands pressed the tiny mouth organ to her lips, as if to catch any faint breath that might escape.

Merry put her hand to her lips. "Michael, is she—"

Michael knelt beside Julie and took one of her bruised hands in his. His fingers were trembling as he felt for her pulse.

"She's all right, Merry. Only fainted, I think."

"What can I do?"

"Get back to the hut as quickly as you can. Tell the boys to come and help me. You get some hot water and warm blankets ready."

Merry nodded, then raced over the rocks the short distance that separated them from the hut.

After the boys ran to join Michael, Merry hurried around the kitchen, putting water on the stove, bringing blankets from the dormitory to warm on lines by the fire. Her heart pounded as she worked.

Soon the boys came in carrying Julie. They removed her sodden raincoat and unlaced her muddy boots. Merry dragged the blankets down from the lines, and they wrapped Julie in them and propped her in a chair near the stove. Michael dashed some cold water in her face.

As Julie's eyelids quivered open, Merry pressed a spoonful of hot milk to Julie's slightly parted lips. A tinge of color appeared on her pale cheeks. Her gray eyes seemed bewildered, but as she focused, a slight smile appeared. Julie's hands also needed care. They were bruised and matted with blood. Michael dipped a cloth in the hot water and gently washed her hands free of dirt and blood. When he finished, Julie made a motion with her fingers as if to write.

"She wants a paper and pencil," one of the boys said.

Merry quickly produced both from one of the kitchen shelves. Julie was barely able to hold the pencil. *Thanks. No voice—much calling*, she wrote.

The four standing around her looked at each other then at the words, uncertain as to their meaning.

"I think she means she lost her voice by calling so much," Michael said.

Julie nodded her head at Michael.

Voices and stamping feet sounded outside the hut. The door opened.

As Julie's eyelids quivered open, Merry pressed a spoonful of hot milk to Julie's slightly parted lips.

"Not a trace anywhere," Bill said, then stopped on the threshold, staring in amazement at the group around the stove. "She's here!"

"We found her just a little while ago and brought her here," Merry said. "She's weak but all right."

A glad confusion of voices filled the hut. The rescue team's weariness and discouragement evaporated. The search had ended successfully, even though they were not the ones who brought it to a close.

Uncle Tony came over and stood beside Merry. "Good work," he said, his smile lifting the tiredness from his face.

"Was it hard going, Uncle Tony?" Michael asked.

He nodded. "Slippery and rough, especially when we were off the trails. We searched the whole ravine. Everyone thought she was there."

"Well done," Bob said. "It doesn't matter who found her as long as she's found."

"But where did you find her?" Bill asked Merry and Michael. "I thought we knew the mountain."

"She was about one hundred yards east of the hut in a sort of cave made by the rocks," Michael explained. "She's been shouting so much she's lost her voice."

"East of the hut!" Bill repeated. "No wonder none of us heard her with the wind blowing so. But how did you hear her?"

"We heard her little mouth organ. She had it pressed to her lips," Merry said.

"Thanks, Britons," Bill held out his hand and shook theirs warmly. "How long have you been in the United States?" he asked with a smile.

"Three days," Merry replied.

"Doesn't take you long to show your stuff, does it?"

Bob grasped their hands in appreciation. "Well, folks," he smiled, "rescues come and go, but meals go on forever, and something tells me that we're all going to be pretty hungry tonight."

Bob and Bill laid aside their mountain gear for white aprons, and Bill stuck a chef's hat on his head. Dishes rattled about the kitchen as strange concoctions came into being.

Merry summoned up her courage, hoping her face would stay straight. "Bob," she began, "I made a pudding for dessert." She handed the baking dish to him. "It should be baked for half an hour."

"Thanks, Merry." He looked at it suspiciously. "It looks good. Maybe it is good."

"What is it?" Bill asked.

"Chocolate nut," Merry said innocently. "It's one of Michael's favorites. I thought the rest of you might like it too."

"Chocolate nut pudding, did you say, Merry?" Michael asked. "That's jolly good news."

Julie remained huddled in her corner by the stove, the warmest place in the hut, and everyone knew she still needed warmth more than anything else. She had no way of communicating with them and was too weak to write properly, but occasionally she would press the tiny mouth organ to her lips to join in the merriment. They laughed and cheered and toasted her with pineapple juice, and she replied with ripples of melody.

When it came time for dessert, Bob placed the steaming mahogany-colored pudding in front of Merry and suggested she serve it. Merry did not dare look up at him in case her smile should give her away. She cut the pudding in slices and poured on each one some of the creamy sauce Bill had whipped up. At the first taste, exclamations of approval raced around the table.

"Oh, boy, can you cook!" Sam commented.

"It's absolutely tops, Merry," Michael said appreciatively. "You never made it so well in London."

The plates came back for second helpings, and soon the pudding dish was empty. Merry began to wonder when, or how, or if ever, she should say anything about the pudding's origin.

"Well, everybody," Bob began teasingly, "how about finishing up with a nice piece of spice cake?"

"Please don't mention that granite slab," Bill said.

"No, really, Bob, I couldn't possibly have any more," Michael protested.

"I'd like some, Bob," Merry looked up. "I liked it yesterday, so why not today? Good things improve with time."

Bob began to search the shelves. "Where is my spice cake?" he muttered to himself. "Did you boys eat it up this afternoon when everyone was out?" he asked Sam and Carl.

"We wouldn't eat that spice cake if we had to starve," they said.

Bob came back to the table after finding nothing. "This hut is getting too full of mysteries for me."

Merry was trying hard not to laugh. Uncle Tony saw her and caught her eye. He winked at her.

"I believe I know where a great deal of that spice cake is, Bob," Tony said slowly, then pointed to Michael's middle.

It took a moment for the truth about the spice cake to sink in, but soon the hut was filled with the sounds of everyone's laughter.

Late that night, Bob and Bill carried Julie into the dormitory where Merry had added extra blankets to Julie's bed to make it more comfortable.

"Good night," they said, and the trail of light made by their lantern disappeared.

Through the window of the dark room, Merry could see a white moon in the heavens and a few scudding clouds in the clear sky. The wind had completely dropped. Merry watched lights far down in the valley twinkling on in the night.

"Good night, Julie," Merry whispered.

The reply of tinkled notes seemed to be the loveliest sound Merry had ever heard.

Chapter 9

The Shadow of the Eagle

Early the next morning, Merry quietly slipped out of her cocoon of blankets. Julie was still asleep. Out the window, she could see sunlight touching the tip of Washington on the north and Monroe on the south. Merry smoothed her clothes and tidied her hair, then picked up her boots to put on outdoors.

She found Michael standing just outside the front door. Merry took a deep breath of the sun-filled air. A haziness dwelt in the atmosphere, but Michael and Merry could clearly see the pale blue of the sky above and the autumn tints of the trees below. The soft outlines of the mountains melted away into infinities of distance.

Michael held a map of the mountain range in his hand. "We've a tremendous long way to go," he said, drawing a path with his finger, "that is, if we go along the Presidential Range and get back to Pinkham tonight. We certainly want to do the first, and we'll have to do the last as Uncle Tony has only another day or two before he has to go back to England."

"Oh—" Merry's voice dropped. She kept forgetting that Uncle Tony was going to leave them. The reminder of that fact was always the wrong kind of surprise.

Bob and Bill were making cheerful sounds with pots and pans in the kitchen. Michael and Merry went inside to fold blankets and pack their rucksacks so they could be ready to leave right after breakfast. Merry found Julie sitting up on the edge of her bunk.

"How are you doing, Julie?" Merry asked.

"I have my voice again. That is something."

"Are you feeling all right?"

"Yes," Julie said with a smile. "With all the sleep I have had, I am well and strong enough to do anything now." Julie held out her hand, and Merry took it.

"Meredith, I do want to thank you and your brother for saving my life yesterday," Julie said hesitantly.

"I'm sure the men would have found you sooner or later, Julie."

"No, Meredith. They had searched where I was. They came so near I could have touched them, but I had no strength. They would not have searched that way again."

"But your music—"

"They did not know what it was. I heard them say it was the wind, just as you and Michael thought it was the mountain streams when you were so near me. But you two kept on until you found me."

Breakfast was another big meal with something to please everyone. There was porridge, bacon, boiled eggs, corn bread and maple syrup, hot chocolate, and coffee. During breakfast, Julie told them of her experience.

"As you know, I left early yesterday morning. I was determined to join my friends at the Base Station, and I was confident that I could do it. I had gone only a short way down the ravine when the wind and rain came up worse than ever. It was impossible to see the path, so I turned back to retrace my steps. I tried to use the rocks for support, but I kept slipping, which is how I bruised my hands and tore my clothes. Once in a while, I could see the outline of the hut and I thought I was going directly toward it, but I never reached it.

"I gave the mountain distress signals, but the wind was too loud for anyone to hear me. I kept fumbling around, calling for help until I no longer had any voice to call with.

Finally, I just sank down among the rocks. I found a small hollow, and I crawled into it for shelter.

"I knew nothing at all until I heard your voices," she nodded to Bill and Bob, "but I could not move and the mist was still thick and the wind so noisy. I thought my music was too soft, but later Michael and Meredith heard me." Julie smiled at them across the table. "I thank you all. I would not have thought anybody cared enough about me to spend the day hunting for me." Her gray eyes filled with tears. She looked down at the table.

Bob patted her shoulder. "Don't worry. It wasn't you we cared about; it was the mountain. We didn't want it to lose its good reputation!"

Everyone laughed as they pushed their chairs back from the table. All except Merry and Julie headed to the dormitories to collect their packs since everyone was leaving the hut except Bob and Bill.

Merry leaned toward Julie. "We all care for you, Julie. Everyone does."

Julie looked at her. "Thank you, Meredith. Now I do not feel so lonely. I have always wished I had a brother or a sister. I never even knew my mother."

"Oh, Julie," Merry said in sympathy. She reached out and took Julie's hand in her own. "We could be like sisters while we're both here in America, if you'd like."

Julie's loneliness seemed swept away with her smile. "Yes. Let us be sisters always."

"But, please call me Merry. Everyone else does."

Julie smiled at her. The two girls exchanged addresses, promising to write to each other and perhaps even see each other at Christmas.

Soon the men were coming back into the room, saying goodbye, shaking hands all around. No one of them might ever see any of the others again, but two days in a mountain hut had made all of them comrades for life.

Sam and Carl were eager to leave immediately so they could report back quickly at their jobs. Julie was to travel with them since she needed to return to the base station as well. When Julie and Merry said goodbye, Julie pressed a small package into Merry's hand. "It's just a little gift for my sister."

Merry smiled. "Thank you, Julie. May I open it now?"

Julie shook her head. "No, not now. Not until you hear a bird sing; then you may open it."

"But when—" Merry began to ask.

Bob, who had been standing nearby, supplied the answer. "When you get into the timber, probably not before."

"But that won't be until afternoon!"

"So much the better," Julie laughed.

When the last goodbye had been said, Uncle Tony, Michael, and Merry were on their upward way.

They started off on the trail that led to the summit, but they branched away at a point and took the Westside Trail around Washington. It was slow going over the great boulders and rocks that covered the mountainside, but they had the whole autumn day before them. Washington's peak was visible as they skirted its side, bathed in a radiance of warmth and light.

They scrambled up Mount Clay and saw the Great Gulf, that vast depression between the ridges, yawning below them. A blue haze softened the jagged outlines of rocks and the dark pointed tips of pines. Soon they crossed the Monticello Lawn, so called because it was a wide flat space where stunted grass grew among the boulders. Nearby was a mossy nook where a few balsams grew, their fragrance sweet in the light wind. The red of a cranberry bush flashed in the sun. Long overripe blueberries were growing along the ground.

Uncle Tony told them of the shy wildlife that lived among the boulders: the kangaroo mouse, the curiously brilliant grasshoppers, the rare butterflies that had been found no place else in the world. As he spoke, the shadow of an eagle fell over them, and they looked up to see the great creature with its powerful wings outspread floating leisurely through the sky, following the contour of the mountains.

Merry was trying to put her feelings into words when Michael said them for her.

"Under the shadow of the American eagle, that's where we've come to stay."

They took Mount Jefferson in stride and soon reached the gaunt peak. Uncle Tony broke a chocolate bar in thirds and offered it to Michael and Merry.

"I sometimes wonder why I climb mountains," he said as they rested. "I can never find an answer persuasive enough for one who has no heart for climbing, but I do believe that everyone who climbs is some manner of artist. He must be to appreciate the beauty outspread before him." Michael and Merry nodded in agreement.

The trio soon trod over the ridges and through the passes between mountain peaks, keeping to the Gulfside Trail, passing a whole family of mountains—Mount Adams, Mount Sam Adams, and Mount John Quincy Adams. Veering more to the west, the eastern valley which they had been looking down into all morning was soon cut off by a granite wall, and the western valley unrolled before them. Their stopping-place for lunch was before them now—Madison Hut, lying at the base of the pyramid-peaked Mount Madison.

The hut men had seen them coming and were in the process of preparing a good lunch for the climbers. After an hour's rest and a stalwart meal, Uncle Tony, Michael, and Merry felt ready for anything and started off again.

The Madison Trail rose sharply. Merry looked down at the hut and saw it as if it were an elf's cottage. The rocks they crawled over were enormous, looking as if they might topple over at any moment, although in actuality they had been locked to the mountain for so long that they had become part of the mountain. The rocks' rough surfaces and ample holds gave the mountain the same ladder-like rise that Lion Head had given. It was a difficult climb, but Uncle Tony, Michael, and Merry reached the peak so soon that the work was forgotten in the majesty of the height. The peak rose sharply into sky. The view to the north swept over ridges that fell away to lowlands and villages and industrial centers; east and west to the flat green ribbons of valleys that rose up to distant ranges; south over the long way they had come since morning around the impressive bulk of Washington.

Then their climb down began, a downward slant that would not change until they were safe in the valley. They took the Osgood Trail, a knife-like ridge with spectacular views on either side. The sun was still high, the day still warm with a softening haze. As they approached timber, they could see the checkered effect of the hand of autumn on the mountainside—the dark pines mixed with the flaming brilliance of scarlet maples and the golden richness of a cluster of birches. When they entered the timber, the path became a smooth way over the uneven earth. The long patches of mossy earth made the climbers feel as if they were walking on clouds. Brooks trickled down the mountain from springs that sent their freshness into the valley. The trees grew larger as the trio descended, and more birches, beeches, and maples appeared among the pines.

A red squirrel looked down at them, chattering indignantly at their intrusion into his solitude. Distantly, a low whisper of twigs proclaimed a deer's flight. A sudden song sounded from a neighboring tree, and they looked up to see a bright wood bird.

"Now I can open Julie's present!" Merry exclaimed. With eager hands she took the package from her pocket and unwrapped it, discovering the tiny mouth organ. Merry put it to her lips and tinkled a reply to the bird above who cocked his head before answering with a quizzical note.

"I wondered if it would be that," Uncle Tony smiled.

"Oh, but Uncle Tony," Merry said, "she really shouldn't have done it."

"Perhaps not," he answered, "but she probably felt that it would not have been much good to her later if you and Michael had not heard it when you did."

"I do like it," Merry said, pocketing it carefully.

Michael broke up a chocolate bar and offered it around. "It looks to me on the map as if we still have a long way to go," he remarked, "and the sun doesn't have much time left in the sky."

For the next two hours, their descent into the valley was a race with darkness. They knew by the map that there was a good-sized mountain stream—a branch of the Peabody River—to cross. Their eyes began to fail to pierce the swiftly gathering dusk, but their ears caught the sound of the stream in the distance and led them to it. They swiftly crossed the small suspension bridge that was slung across the raging waters and found the trail marker fixed to a tree on the opposite shore.

The path was boggy in places since they were at valley level. The dark evening air seemed moist, and the heavy shroud of woods enclosing them gave no views of peaks or ridges. They traveled at a light trot, their packs jouncing on their backs, and though they could not see the trail because of the enfolding darkness, they somehow never got off it. They did not speak, and the earth muffled their steps, so the

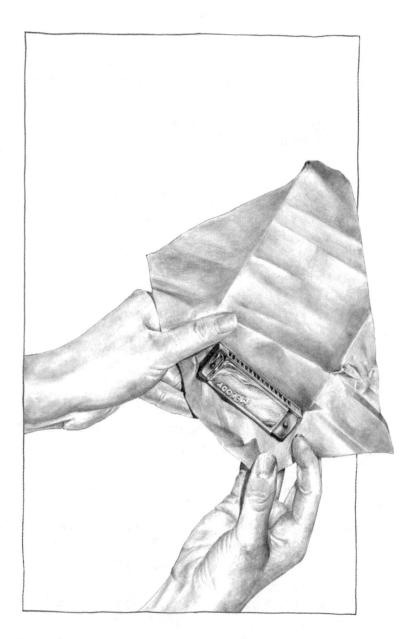

*With eager hands, Merry took the package from her pocket
and unwrapped it, discovering the tiny mouth organ.*

silence was unbroken except for a distant crackling of twigs as a creature crept near to gaze with darkness-accustomed eyes at the three fleet figures only a little darker than the forest gloom.

Merry began to wonder how much farther they could go before night would force them to a stop while Michael tried to think of ways to improvise a shelter. But Uncle Tony led on, keeping them to the path as a skipper would keep a boat to its course.

They could soon hear the sound of traffic threading the valley road. Then, through the spaces in the trees, they saw the twinkle of lights in nearby farmhouses. They came into the clearing, a wide, flat meadowland bordering the river, and the light and sound seemed like outstretched hands of welcome.

A wisp of light still lingered in the sky, and after they had put a small distance between themselves and the woods, they could look back and see their day etched against the coming stars. There was the great bulk of Washington, so broad and strong, the sharp cone of Madison, and the ridge leading from the peak to the timber.

Their legs felt stiff on the level land after the insistent downward plunge of the afternoon, but they kept going along the wide and clear valley road. Lights winked from the houses, and mist rose from the river. The range of mountains around them seemed like a great protecting arm across the land. The reflection of the stars overhead quivered in the river as the current swept on.

"Mum and Daddy are looking at those same stars," Merry said as they continued along. "Perhaps if everyone looked at the stars, we would know more about peace."

"That's a good thought, Merry, for there's always wisdom in the long perspective," said Uncle Tony.

Soon the lights of the camp at Pinkham Notch were before their eyes. Then they were on the porch, heaving off rucksacks, and Pippin was in their arms, wriggling with joy to have them back again.

Chapter 10
A Letter and a Goodbye

Uncle Tony, Michael, and Merry left early the next morning, driving south through the autumn sunshine and rolling hills to the New England village that would be Michael and Merry's home for an unknown period of time. The larger hills sloped down to smaller ones as they drove through a country where autumn was a gilded glory rather than a leisurely transition as in England. Late in the afternoon they came to their village, just one neat street shaded by golden maples. There were many small white houses interspersed with an occasional stately red brick house. There was a post office, a store or two, a public library, a school, and at the end of the street a gracious white church with classic, simple lines.

Michael had a guidebook on the seat beside him, and as they had gone along he had read interesting facts to them about the different villages. He looked up at the church with a pleased exclamation.

"It has a Christopher Wren spire," he told them, gazing at the graceful white steeple. He did not feel so far from London now that the New England village they were to live in had a spire like those of many London churches.

Merry read further in the guidebook. "It also has a Paul Revere bell," she said. The two features seemed to be a good sign. If an Englishman's idea and an American's craftsmanship could abide in such hourly harmony as a striking bell in

There was a post office, a store or two, a public library, a school, and at the end of the street a gracious white church with classic, simple lines.

a towering steeple, then there was some hope for herself and Michael to fit into the pattern of this new land.

Uncle Tony inquired at the post office for directions to his friends' house, and they were soon driving along a lovely winding road with an archway of interlacing boughs and a carpet of crinkled fallen leaves. They crossed noisy brooks and went past sleepy farmhouses. Cattle grazed contentedly in the meadows. Black-faced and black-legged sheep nibbled at the grass.

They soon reached a little house perched on a tiny hill like a cherry on a sundae. Its name, Hilltop, was lettered on the mailbox. A great maple blazing with color stood by the house, and a little path bordered by flowers led up to its welcoming front door. As Uncle Tony brought the car to a stop, the door was flung open, and a jolly, gray-haired man came down the path.

"Antony!" he exclaimed as they shook hands, and in their few words of greeting all the years they had not seen each other rolled away.

"Tom, I want you to meet my niece and nephew, Meredith and Michael Lamb."

Tom Greenwood shook their hands. "You've never met my wife, Tony," Tom said as a woman came down the path. "Kate, this is my old friend, Antony Lamb."

Kate warmly greeted Uncle Tony, then turned quickly to Merry and Michael. Merry held out her hand formally, but that would not do for the quiet-voiced woman with a gentle face. She put her arms around Merry and held her tight for a moment.

"Dear child," she said simply, "we're so glad you have come to stay with us for a while."

Michael grew red with embarrassment, hoping he would not have to be hugged. But Kate Greenwood knew better. She held out her hand to him, and he took it with a smile of relief.

"Do you think you could possibly give our dog a home too?" Merry asked.

"Why, of course!" Kate answered swiftly. "We've always wanted a dog, we've always wanted a boy and girl, and now we've got them all at once." She bent down and patted Pippin, then she turned to her husband. "Tom, let the bags wait for a bit. Tea is ready now. We can come get them later."

She turned and took Merry's arm, and they started up the path to the wide-open front door. Merry found that she did not feel as lonely as she had been sure that she would feel. As she stepped over the threshold, she felt as if she had entered a place that felt almost like home.

"Does everyone call you Merry?" Kate Greenwood asked.

"Oh, yes," Merry smiled, and Kate saw why.

"What would you call me if you were in England?"

Merry hesitated a moment, then felt her shyness slip away. "We would call you Auntie Kate and Uncle Tom," she said. "That's what we call all Daddy's and Mum's good friends."

"Then will you call us that?"

Michael smiled and nodded. "Certainly!"

"Of course, Auntie Kate," Merry answered.

"Tony," Kate asked, "you are staying the night, aren't you?"

"I wish I could," he replied, "but I've got only just enough time to get back to Montreal before the ship is due to sail. I'll stay till after supper, if I may, and then drive all night."

A cheerful fire burned on the hearth, and soon Kate spread tea before them. It was an American tea with cinnamon toast and dark chocolate cake, which Michael and Merry both pronounced excellent.

"We lead a quiet life here," Tom began. "After London, I don't know what you two will think of it."

"There's lots of work for willing hands," Kate added, "in the house, in the garden, and in the woods."

"We'd be happy to help," Michael said, and Merry nodded her agreement.

"I don't know whether the village school will be much in the way of education," Tom said.

"Do they have chemistry?" Michael asked.

The Greenwoods looked at each other and shook their heads.

"Oh, that's all right," Michael said quickly.

"Please don't be concerned about that, Tom," Uncle Tony assured him. "It means a great deal just now for the children to have a home in America. My brother and his wife are trying to find a way to send money out of England so Michael and Merry can go to boarding schools, but so far that hasn't proved possible. I'm sure the school will be quite adequate for a while anyway."

Tom threw another birch log on the fire, and the white bark flamed brightly.

"Did that come from your own woods?" Uncle Tony asked.

Tom shook his head. "These logs were something of a gift. Fine, dry wood, too."

"Tell them about it, Tom," Kate urged.

"Well, down in the village there's a man named Dunton who has a portable saw. He makes his living by toting it around to different homes and sawing up people's wood into fireplace lengths. A short while ago, the truck on which he carries his saw caught fire. He didn't have any way of putting it out or sounding an alarm, so it burned flat, and he was left with the bleak outlook of no means of making any money to buy a new one."

"What did he do?" Michael asked.

"It got around the village, and people began to put their heads together, and before you knew it a fund was started for him. We raised enough to buy him a whole new outfit—even better than his old one—and he was so grateful that he went around and sawed and stacked a cord of wood for everyone.

"Fire is the hazard in this countryside," Tom continued, "and these days, with the woods so dry and brittle, we are always on the lookout."

"Do you have good fire protection?" Uncle Tony asked.

"Splendid. All voluntary. We hear the siren go, and we all rush in the direction its blasts indicate and work together."

The word "siren" reminded Merry of something.

"How is London?" she asked.

The Greenwoods exchanged glances with each other.

"It's been several days since we've seen a newspaper or heard any news," Uncle Tony added quickly, "and no letters have come since we landed. We'd all rather like to know how London is."

"London has stood up magnificently," Tom said. "The people are all heroes, but the city has been battered terribly, night after night."

He handed a newspaper to the three guests. The headlines were enough. Michael and Merry stared at them. Merry felt a cold shuddering horror, but she knew this too was one of the things they had to be brave enough to face. It was awful to feel that she was safe when all she loved was in hourly danger of utter and terrible destruction. But the time would come, as it had come in the situation with Julie, when she and Michael could do their part. Merry felt herself stiffen with resolve.

"They will come out all right," she murmured.

Kate rose. "Come and let me show you to your rooms."

Michael and Merry followed her up the stairs to two tiny rooms, side by side, waiting for them. Michael's room had a window facing north, up the hill and into the pine woods. Kate informed him that he would have a good view of any deer that might emerge from the woods. The window in Merry's room faced east. *I can look toward England*, she thought as she gazed into the distance.

They brought their luggage up and spent the next hour getting settled. Tom and Uncle Tony went for a walk and brought back the evening mail from the village. With a big smile, Uncle Tony handed a letter from England to Michael and Merry.

They opened it in eagerness while Tom and Kate discreetly disappeared. Some of the paragraphs were written by Daddy and some by Mum. Merry read the letter aloud.

Dear Michael and Merry,

Things have been terrible here in London ever since you left, and we wouldn't want to tell you anything less. The nights—and even many of the days—have been shattering. Bombs have fallen very near us. The houses at the end of the street are gone, and our front door and windows have buckled under the strain. The blackout has been lit at night by the glow of fires. The streets are littered, and our hearts break to see such wanton destruction. But we always remind ourselves of two things: that you are safe, carrying on for us and for Britain, and that buildings are only things, no matter how lovely, and can be replaced.

Everyone is doing his part to help—there is so much kindness and helpfulness in those around us. Everyone is a hero, from the fighters who write their deeds in the sky to the dustmen sweeping debris from the streets.

Whatever you read of the wonderful spirit of the Londoners is not exaggerated, and we are proud to share in it to a small degree. We do not wish to be in any place but London right now, but we would not wish you to be any place else than where you are. Of course we often get frightened. When an aerial torpedo whistles overhead or a landmine thumps at the end of the street, our knees feel wobbly but our hearts are stout. And everyone here realizes that though our bodies may be endangered, our hearts are free, and they shall remain free. But we could not be so happy if we did not know you were safe.

We hope you are feeling at home in America. Honor the flag that is protecting you, for it is the flag of freedom, wav-

ing beside the Union Jack in all the support it is giving us. And we know that on whatever side of the Atlantic we may be we are together in our thoughts. Nothing that happens anywhere can take that haven from us.

We send both of you our love, and we promise that you will have as much reason to be proud of us as we have to be proud of you.

Love and kisses,
Mum and Daddy

"I wish there were something we could do to help them," Michael said as Merry tucked the letter into the envelope.

"You are helping them," Uncle Tony said quietly, "and you will continue to. Life gives opportunities to those who can take them. And I think that both you and Merry can take them."

The Greenwoods called them in to supper in the little pine-paneled dining room. The candles threw soft shadows on the walls, casting a glow of peace. Merry did not feel guilty any longer at having beauty and comfort around her, for Mum and Daddy had said that thinking of her and Michael in such surroundings helped them.

And then supper was over, and Uncle Tony pulled on his coat, and no one could say when they might be meeting again. They said goodbye on the doorstep. Merry hugged her uncle tightly, and Michael shook his hand firmly. Uncle Tony walked to the car, switched on the lights, and started the engine.

"There's always a mountain to climb!" he called back to them as he gave a last wave. Then the car rolled smoothly down the road.

"When do you think we will see him again?" Merry asked.

"When the war is over," Michael said.

They turned back to the house.

Inside, the Greenwoods suggested quietly that Michael and Merry must be tired after such a long day and that perhaps they would like to go to their rooms early. Michael and Merry thanked them, said goodnight, and headed up the stairs to their little rooms with Pippin following them.

Chapter 11

A Medal for Pippin

Michael and Merry soon fit into the pattern of village life although they found some things to be different from what they had known in England. Michael played baseball and football on the school team but found both to be strange substitutes for rugby, while Merry learned to apply her hockey skills from England to basketball in America. They had no need for their old school blazers, so they tucked them away in a bottom drawer, and they both soon realized that afternoon tea was more of an occasional event than a regular practice. Sometimes it was hard to understand the new way of speaking English, but they consoled themselves in private that they were holding off an American accent.

There was, however, much that was wonderful. The weather was glorious, and the countryside was fresh and untamed. Indian summer was upon them, that space of mellowness between the first frosts and the rigors of winter. Everyone in the village worked hard for the war relief—sewing, knitting, raising money—and sent cases of clothes and other needed things overseas. Merry and Michael joined Scouts and were able to do their part to help.

Michael continued to train Pippin, teaching him new words and new ways of usefulness. Each morning he walked to school with Michael and Merry, and then at a signal from Michael, he would turn and run back to Hilltop. Michael and Merry often tied notes for Kate to Pippin's collar and urged him to speed back with them. Kate would watch for his arrival, and soon they had Pippin timed to the split second.

One Friday morning, when the spell of summer weather seemed as if it would never be broken, Tom Greenwood said at breakfast, "How about climbing our mountain this afternoon? There's no school tomorrow to worry about."

Michael and Merry's faces lit up. Ever since they had arrived, they had been longing to climb the rounded mountain that rose above meadows and pine woods, sheltering Hilltop from northwest winds.

"We don't get home from school until nearly four o'clock. Will we be able to reach the summit and return before dark?" Michael asked.

"Well," Tom Greenwood smiled slowly, "I thought we might spend the night up there and come down tomorrow."

"Oh, Uncle Tom!" they exclaimed. In all of their mountain adventures with Uncle Tony, they had never camped overnight on a mountaintop.

"Just imagine," Merry said, her eyes dancing, "waking up in the morning and having the whole earth and sky and miles and miles of beautiful view for your bedroom!"

"Can we build a fire and cook our supper?" Michael asked.

Tom shook his head. "I don't think so. There's been no rain for weeks, and the woods are dry as tinder. The fire warden probably wouldn't let us, and we wouldn't want to ask him."

"There was a fire in the Roberts' field yesterday," Kate said.

"Were they able to put it out?" Merry asked.

"Yes, just short of the woods."

"Good thing. If it had got into their timber it might still be burning," Tom said.

"What started it?" Michael asked.

Kate shrugged her shoulders. "A careless hunter, they think, on his way across the fields into the woods."

"There are certainly a lot of dangers," Merry said, thinking of the unpredictable weather on Mount Washington and now the constant risk of fire in the woods.

The school hours dragged slowly. But finally afternoon did come, and then four o'clock, and soon they were standing in the kitchen helping Kate put sandwiches, fruit, and thermos bottles into their rucksacks. They changed quickly into their climbing gear, then pulled their rucksacks onto their shoulders along with their blanket rolls.

Kate waved to them from the kitchen door as they went down the path, Pippin at their heels. "See you for breakfast," Kate called after them. They waved back, then the road took her from their sight. The round slope of the mountain loomed before them, its feet in the pines, its head in the clouds.

"You may have to keep Pippin close to you, Michael," Tom warned, "because sheep may still be grazing on the mountain."

Tom Greenwood was more of a woodsman than a mountaineer, so they had much to exchange with each other as they walked along the country road to the lane which turned off and led toward the sheep pastures. Overhead, white birches linked their arms with gray beeches; the thick leaves on the path made a rustling music as they scuffed through them.

"Why do you suppose people ever left this beautiful place to go West?" Merry asked.

"Many reasons," Tom replied. "Perhaps their well went dry, perhaps the frosts came too early for them to make a profit from their farming, perhaps the lure of the land when the West opened up was too much for them. These rocky New England fields made a farmer's life far from easy."

They passed through a gate, and the trail opened to a hillside with scattered boulders and pines. Sheep grazed in these pastures and looked up at the trio curiously as they passed. Tom pointed up the mountain.

"If we keep our eyes on the highest line of balsams, we should be heading straight enough."

They went on, and as they started climbing up the mountain, the sun started climbing down the sky. They pressed upward where the grass gave way to rocks and the oaks and maples gave place to pines. The setting sun was warm, and their rucksacks and blanket rolls were heavy, but at last they reached the ridge of balsams. The sharp scent of the trees filled the air. Merry, Michael, and Tom stopped for breath and looked back.

The hillside pitched steeply, sweeping down past the grazing sheep to a valley dark with forests and blue with lakes, sweeping up again to the brooding mass of Monadnock against the southern sky. The great mountain that seemed to gather all the lesser hills in its embrace looked like a mother hen gathering her chicks under her wings. To the east and the west, they glimpsed more distant peaks.

"Will we reach the top of the mountain in time to catch the sunset?" Merry asked.

Tom nodded. "If we hurry. There's just a bit more to do."

They hastened on over moss and boulders and over an old, rambling stone wall. The mountaintop marker came into sight, and Michael and Merry raced to it, laying their hands on its rough sides and congratulating each other on a reaching another peak.

They worked quickly to set up camp for the night. They found a smooth granite slab on which to eat their supper and watch the sunset. They sat together in silence facing the west. The sun seemed to balance on the rim of the world as the light deepened from rose to gold. There was a brief space of twilight, of color spreading and fading, of distant blue ranges melting away into bluer distances so that the known world seemed to clasp hands with the unknown.

Lights came on in the valley, some low in the valley linked by a ribbon of road, others halfway up the mountains. Stars flickered in the sky, and a soft breeze blew from the northwest.

"It's cold, isn't it?" Merry said, shivering a little as she pulled on her jacket. "But this rock still feels warm."

"Granite holds the sun's warmth long after the sun has gone," Tom said. "But let's get into our blanket rolls before we get cold."

They crept deep down among their blankets, trying to tuck up any slit where the searching air of night might enter. It was hard to persuade Pippin that this was the time for sleep. He sat beside them wide awake, ears pricked as he caught the night sounds—the bleating of sheep, the trilling of insects, the clock in the village that told the hours throughout the night. Michael, Merry, and Tom talked quietly for a few moments, and then silence enfolded them.

Merry awakened last the next morning and found Tom and Michael's blanket rolls in crumpled heaps. Merry got to her feet and smoothed the wrinkles in her clothes. A strange smell drifted on the morning air, and Merry stiffened. It was a hot, dusty smell, a smell of burning. She looked around but saw nothing. Then she caught a glimpse of Michael and Tom coming up the mountain.

"Come quickly!" she shouted, waving her arms.

She raced down the slope to meet them halfway.

"We went to the spring to find water," Michael said breathlessly.

"It's dry as a bone," Tom added.

Merry grabbed their hands. "Come quickly to the top! I think I smell fire!"

Tom stared at her and then sprinted to the summit. Michael and Merry followed and stood beside him as he surveyed the countryside. The smell of smoke filled the air, and they could see a veil of smoke like a thin, wispy hand wafting up from far down the mountain.

"A forest fire," Tom muttered. "We've got to fight it. We can try beating it with blankets—perhaps it's not too much underway."

They grabbed their blankets and packs and sped down the mountainside. The closer they got, the denser the clouds of smoke became. They could hear the fire crackling in the dried juniper, sizzling along the leaves of the forest floor.

"We're going to need help," Tom said. "Michael, you run—" He stopped short. It would take Michael the better part of an hour to reach the village and would deprive them of a firefighter in the meantime.

Pippin whimpered at the sight of the flames. Laying his ears back, he lifted one of his front paws pitifully.

"Pippin can go for help!" Michael shouted. "Hurry, write a note to Auntie Kate."

Tom scribbled a note. *Get fire engine—quick—east side of mountain burning—lay hose to water hole.*

Merry stuck her handkerchief in her mouth and got it wet. She tied the note in the handkerchief before tying it to Pippin's collar in case he went close to the flames. Then Michael held Pippin's head between his hands and looked him straight in the eyes.

"Pippin, run to Autie Kate. Run to Hilltop!" With the last word, he released Pippin.

Pippin hesitated for a second to get his bearings, then in a rush he was off through the woods, skirting the fire.

"He'll get the message through," Michael said.

They seized their blankets and beat them along the edge of the fire, trying to keep it from spreading over the dry ground, trying to localize it—beating, dodging the fire here, following it there, gulping smoke and coughing, stopping for a second to wipe their smarting eyes, then going at it again.

They went past weariness and became machines. They forgot when they had started or if they would ever stop. The flames roared before them, shooting up high into the trees. Then, like weird music, they heard the fire siren in the village, rising and falling even above the hiss and roar of the flames.

The siren echoed into silence. Soon they heard the bell of the fire engine as it sped over the curving country road. Through a gap in the trees, they could just glimpse the engine stopping at the water hole in the valley, attaching its long hose and getting the pumps in action. There seemed to be a dozen men, pulling on fire fighting gear, starting up the mountain with spades and axes, dragging the hose behind them.

Tom and Michael and Merry beat on in spite of their aching arms and stinging eyes. Then a stream of water played on the trees. They cheered with throats so parched that only a small sound came through. There was a sizzling snap, then the flames seemed to shoot higher and more viciously than ever. Men fought their way into the woods, cutting into the brush, digging trenches. The water rose and fell, and the flames began to yield.

How long it all took no one knew, but the moment came when they stood in the midst of sodden skeletons of trees, the blackened earth smoldering, and the fire out. For all its violence and noise, the area of destruction was comparatively small. The men mopped their faces and put their heads under the running hose.

Merry cupped her hands for a drink, holding the cool water in her dry mouth.

"You got the message we sent?" Michael hoarsely asked the fire chief.

The chief smiled. "Sure did, son. Mrs. Greenwood telephoned us that you were in trouble. The message came early, so most of the men were still in the village. Five minutes later and they'd have gotten off to their work, and it wouldn't have been so easy for them to get here quickly. That's some dog you have."

Michael smiled proudly. "Thank you."

The chief turned to Tom Greenwood. "You did well keeping it down, Tom. It hasn't burned much good stuff, but if it had gotten into that stand of pines it would have been a bad loss."

"How do you think it started?" Tom asked.

"Your guess is as good as mine." The chief shrugged his shoulders. "I suspect it was carelessness, most likely a hunter."

"We've got to find a way to help people respect these woods more," Tom said.

The chief assigned two men to stay on the spot in case the fire broke out again, and the rest prepared to go down the mountain. Michael and Merry rode on the front seat beside the chief. The men would return to their jobs as postmen, store clerks, farmers, and carpenters, but every one of them would be ready to answer another emergency if the siren should sound.

The fire engine came to a noisy stop in front of Hilltop. Clutching their packs, Michael, Merry, and Tom climbed down and waved as the fire engine drove away.

"How is Pippin?" they asked quickly when Kate greeted them at the door.

"He's all right. A bit tired, but quite pleased with himself."

They hurried into the kitchen. Pippin was lying in his basket under the stove. At the sound of their voices, he lifted his head and wagged his tail.

"Oh, Pippin!" Merry exclaimed in sympathy, dropping down on her knees beside him. The hair was singed on one whole side of his lean brown body. There were cuts on his legs that Kate had washed clean, and his left paw was bandaged.

"Well," Michael murmured, kneeling beside the basket, "if any dog ever paid his debt to the world, Pippin has."

Chapter 12

Christmas in America

Soon the bright beauty of autumn had passed, and the first snow came. The contours of the hills and mountains were softened by the white covering. Shadows lay long in the woods, and there was a great silence everywhere. Even the brooks were hushed. Only by standing very still could their prattle be heard under the ice that covered them. At night the stars shone brilliantly, and the air creaked with cold. In the mornings there were tracks of deer, rabbits, and foxes in the snow across the fields and around the house.

As Michael and Merry walked to school each morning, the snow crunched under their feet and their cheeks tingled from the brisk wind. At school, preparations were underway for the Christmas play to be performed early in December. The teachers and students had wanted it to be all their own this year and had asked Merry to write the play since she was a visitor and did so well in her English classes.

"But I don't know what to write it about," Merry stammered in a confusion of joy the day the honor fell on her.

"Just tell the Christmas story in your own words," Miss Gordan said.

Walking home that afternoon, she asked Michael to help her. They had nearly reached Hilltop when Michael had an idea.

"Merry, remember that legend that Dad and Mum told us when they came back from their holiday in Cornwall last year?"

She nodded. "You mean the one about the spider?"

"Yes."

"I think that will be good. I'll try it and read it to you in the morning."

Michael and Merry went to their rooms soon after supper as they did every night when they had homework to do or letters to write. Merry worked busily, filling sheet after sheet with her round handwriting.

Later that night, when they should have had their lights out, Merry crept into Michael's room and read him what she had written. "I can't wait until morning," she whispered. "Can you listen now?"

"Of course. I can't wait to hear it."

When she finished reading the play, Michael nodded. "It's nice, Merry."

"Do you think people will like spiders a little better after seeing it?"

Michael laughed. "Perhaps."

At breakfast the next morning, Kate asked Michael and Merry when the play would be.

"Two weeks from this Saturday," Merry said, "and we've got to work on it ever so quickly to get it ready."

"Merry wrote it last night," Michael announced.

"Oh, my!" Kate exclaimed. "So it's the first performance ever."

"Seems as if we ought to have a bit of a celebration after the performance," Tom added. "We don't have playwrights in our village very often."

"Is there anyone you'd like to ask to come and see it and come back here to supper later?" Kate asked.

"Could I ask Julie? Perhaps she could come since it's to be on a Saturday."

"Of course, but how would she get here?"

"Perhaps her father could bring her."

Merry sent a letter off to Julie that very morning, and a few days later Julie sent a reply saying that they would try to come. At school, the work for the play continued. Parts were cast, lines learned, scenery painted, and costumes made, all by the students themselves under Miss Gordan's direction.

At last, the Saturday afternoon came, a white and snowy one early in December. The program began with carols by the younger students, some folk dances, and a duet. Then the curtains were drawn. Miss Gordan stepped out before the audience.

"We are now presenting a play which has been written by one of our British guests, Meredith Lamb. It is based on an old Cornish legend. The characters are ones you are familiar with—Mary and Joseph, shepherds and kings, soldiers and animals—and the scene is Bethlehem."

The curtain opened slightly, and Merry came to stand beside Miss Gordan. She was tall and slim in a dark wool dress with a white collar and wide blue sash. The crowd applauded, and Merry bowed slightly. Then she smiled broadly, for there on the front row was Julie, and beside her was a distinguished looking man who must be her father. Julie gave a small wave to Merry.

The curtains drew together, and Merry took her seat beside Michael. Soon the curtains parted again, revealing the interior of the stable.

The play progressed smoothly, telling the legend of the spider that spun a web over the bed of the Christ-child to conceal him from the soldiers who wished to destroy the newborn King. At the end, all the students gathered on the platform to sing "O Little Town of Bethlehem."

The lights in the hall came on, and the students came from the platform to mingle with the audience. Kate congratulated Merry on her splendid play, and Tom introduced Michael to Julie's father, Professor von Tiefel. Michael and the professor were soon deep in discussion.

Later that evening, Julie and her father sat with the Greenwoods, Michael, and Merry in front of the fire popping popcorn and discussing some exciting plans that had just been made. Professor von Tiefel said that he would recommend Michael for a scholarship in the preparatory school at which he taught and that a place would be made for Merry in a boarding school near Julie's college. Michael and Merry were thrilled and thanked the professor with bright smiles.

Kate smiled at them both. "We'll miss you so much, but you'll be with us at the holidays, and what an education you'll be receiving to help you when you go back to England!"

The fire gradually dropped from red coals to white ashes. Pippin curled into a ball in front of the fire and was soon fast asleep. Michael and Merry took Julie outside to show her the moonlit outlines of the mountains in the distance. Then they walked back to the house through the snowy countryside with the stars winking overhead and Merry playing carols on the tiny mouth organ.